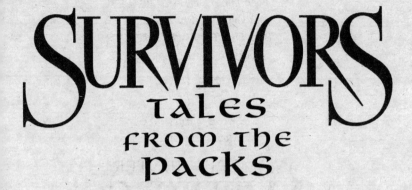

SURVIVORS
TALES FROM THE PACKS

SURVIVORS

Also by ERIN HUNTER

WARRIORS

THE NEW PROPHECY

POWER OF THREE
Book One: The Sight
Book Two: Dark River
Book Three: Outcast
Book Four: Eclipse
Book Five: Long Shadows
Book Six: Sunrise

OMEN OF THE STARS
Book One: The Fourth Apprentice
Book Two: Fading Echoes
Book Three: Night Whispers
Book Four: Sign of the Moon
Book Five: The Forgotten Warrior
Book Six: The Last Hope

DAWN OF THE CLANS
Book One: The Sun Trail
Book Two: Thunder Rising
Book Three: The First Battle
Book Four: The Blazing Star
Book Five: A Forest Divided

EXPLORE THE
WARRIORS WORLD

Warriors Super Edition: Firestar's Quest
Warriors Super Edition: Bluestar's Prophecy
Warriors Super Edition: SkyClan's Destiny
Warriors Super Edition: Crookedstar's Promise
Warriors Super Edition: Yellowfang's Secret
Warriors Super Edition: Tallstar's Revenge
Warriors Super Edition: Bramblestar's Storm
Warriors Field Guide: Secrets of the Clans

SEEKERS

SURVIVORS

TALES FROM THE PACKS

INCLUDES
Alpha's Tale
Sweet's Journey
Moon's Choice

ERIN HUNTER

HARPER
An Imprint of HarperCollinsPublishers

Tales from the Packs
Alpha's Tale, Sweet's Journey, Moon's Choice
Copyright © 2014, 2015 by Working Partners Limited
Series created by Working Partners Limited
www.harpercollinschildrens.com
Library of Congress Control Number: 2015933469
ISBN 978-0-06-229154-7
15 16 17 18 19   CG/OPM   10 9 8 7 6 5 4 3 2 1
❖
Originally published as digital novellas

Special thanks to Gillian Philip

CONTENTS

ALPHA'S TALE

PACK LIST

THE WOLF PACK (IN ORDER OF RANK)

ALPHA:

powerful female with a pale coat and yellow eyes

BETA:

male with shaggy gray fur

BOLD—male with light gray fur

FLEET—smaller male with brown-and-cream fur

NOBLE—female with brown-and-gray fur

QUICK—young male with gray fur and yellow eyes (pup of Graceful, half brother to Pup)

WISE—older male with tawny fur

GRACEFUL—female with gray fur (mother to Quick and Pup)

BRAVE—young male with dark gray fur

DARING—young female with gray-and-cream fur

STRIDENT—young male with dark gray fur

OMEGA:

frail and ancient female with light gray fur

PUP:

PUP—young male with gray-and-white fur and yellow eyes, not yet Named (pup of Graceful, half brother to Quick)

LONGPAW FANGS (IN ORDER OF RANK)

ALPHA:

large black-and-brown male (also known as Sundance)

BETA:

smaller black-and-tan male (also known as Zorro)

BELLE—black-and-tan female

CALAMITY—young black-and-tan female

LONE DOGS

SNAIL—male pup with long ears and shaggy brown fur

CHAPTER ONE

If Pup narrowed his yellow eyes against the sun-dazzle on the snow, he could imagine he was stalking a great deer.

He moved through the trees like a shadow, placing his pads carefully so as not to crunch on exposed pine needles. One paw raised, he froze, pricking an ear forward. An icy breeze blew his prey's scent to his nostrils, rippling his mane of fur, which was almost as thick now as an adult wolf's. Pup lowered his muzzle, snuffing silently at the crust of snow. *Soon it'll be a real deer,* he thought, *or even a giantfur. I could take either of them.*

He was close to becoming a full adult of the Pack. Then he would bring down huge prey with his comrades. *This is how I'll stalk. This is how I'll defend us all against the bite of the long cold.* Pup shifted a paw, edging sideways to remain downwind of the creature. *I'll bring many deer to the Pack to fatten our bellies for Ice Wind.*

Red fur flashed again between the pine trunks, a few

wolf-strides ahead. *Yes, deer,* he thought hungrily. *And elk and mountain goats and . . .*

The creature he was stalking sat up on its tiny hind legs, sniffing the air for prey of its own.

. . . Or weasels. Oh well. Pup breathed a silent sigh. *Keep your mind on the prey at hand, Pup.*

After tonight it would be different. After tonight he would run with the Pack's hunters. After tonight, he would have his Name.

In the dense forest Pup couldn't see the horizon, but he knew where it lay, and he gazed longingly in its direction. That was where the full moon would rise tonight; that was where the Pack would gather and give him his Wolf Name. Impatience and excitement churned in his belly: What would it be? Because *Pup* was nothing. *Pup* was the name given to all young wolves. His true Name would be given to him for his ferocity, perhaps, or his tracking skills, or the long strides he took as he ran. *Longstride.* He liked that. . . .

But it was not his choice. His Pack would name him, and that was as it should be. He felt his tail lift with pride, and then it slumped back, and he blinked.

The weasel—I lost it!

A growl rumbled in his throat, but he held it there. *You fool! If you're not going to be Pup anymore, stop acting like one.* Determinedly he lowered his muzzle to the ground and paced silently forward, nosing out the sharp tang that would lead him back to his prey.

There! Pup went still again, lowering his shoulders. The weasel was sniffing around a rabbit burrow, mad with hunger itself, and it didn't see him coming. Pup sprang, snapped, and flung the weasel to the ground.

Not quite dead! It twisted, bared tiny teeth, and bit wildly at his swiping paw, but this time Pup had it. He seized its thin wriggling spine and crunched, feeling it go limp in his jaws.

You should have been a deer. Next time . . .

Pup trotted back up the slope to where the trees thinned out and the snow was deeper. A gray wolf sat there, gazing down at him and holding the corpse of a white rabbit beneath one powerful paw.

"Mother-Wolf." Pup dropped the weasel respectfully before her, and licked her face in greeting.

"Pup. I watched you." His Mother-Wolf, Graceful, caressed his jaw in return. "You're a fine hunter already. But you need to concentrate." She sounded amused rather than angry.

"I know. I was thinking too much about the moon."

"That's not surprising." Graceful's voice was soft and full

7

of affection as they turned together and carried their prey back toward the Pack-den. "I can't believe you've grown so fast, and so strong. Tonight will be the finest in your young life, Pup, and I already know you'll make me proud." She hesitated, glancing back toward the pine forest, and her voice grew quieter. "I know your father would be proud, too. I wish he could be here to witness your Naming Ceremony. I wish your littermates could be here."

Pup felt the old twist of sadness in his belly, but it was muted now. He'd never known his littermates, after all: Too weak to survive, they had died within weeks of their birth. He'd been the strong one. Sometimes he wondered, with a vague longing, how it would have been to grow up in the rough-and-tumble of a big wolf family, with brothers and sisters around him, and a wolf-sire to watch as they learned to play and hunt and fight together.

No. Even if his siblings had lived, there would have been no wolf family, at least not a real one. His father, after all, was no wolf.

Pup nuzzled Graceful as they walked. He wished his Mother-Wolf could be less sad; talking of her lost pups and mate always made her melancholy. She shouldn't think about them—not tonight. Pup was proud, anyway, of his own survival, the sturdy determination that had seen him through. He and Graceful were the family that mattered: the two of them and—of course—the Pack.

The others were resting together in the low golden light of sunset as he and Graceful padded back into their sandstone-walled valley. Wolves sprawled on rocks, soaking up the last of the sun's rays, or play-fought in pairs, or nibbled fleas and ticks from one another's shaggy coats. Some rose to greet Graceful with a lick and a soft whine; many of them didn't. No wolf took any notice of Pup, but he didn't mind. He was used to that. After tonight, he knew, it would be different.

"You take them both to the prey-store," Graceful said, dropping her rabbit and nudging Pup with her nose. "Let them see you contributing your prey to the Pack." Pup gave a whine of happiness and carried both her rabbit and his own weasel to the prey-store, in a small dark cavern beneath the rocks. There was a fine haul there already; hunting had been good, and the Pack would share tonight as they always did.

He was backing out of the shadowy overhang when he heard voices above him. A slab of sandstone jutted out there, catching the last sun, and two older wolves lay on it, gossiping lazily.

"Should be a good Howl tonight," growled one. Bold, Pup realized, recognizing his voice.

"No clouds. The moon will be bright," agreed the other, Fleet. "The Great Wolf will hear our Howl and answer us."

"Pity, in a way," yawned Bold. "The last Howl wasn't such a perfect night, when Strident and Daring got their names. And tonight it's that half-breed runt's turn."

Pup went still, his blood running cold in his veins.

"Oh, it hardly matters," said Fleet. "Whatever Name he gets, it won't be of any consequence. He'll be Omega soon enough."

"True." Bold gave a rumbling grunt. "How did a wolf like Graceful take up with a filthy dog, anyway?" he muttered. "No wonder most of the pups died."

Pup felt his heart shrink inside him. He crept from the prey-store, his flanks pressed close to the rock wall until he was safely out of sight of the two elders. He knew what the Pack thought of him; he should be used to it. Yet each time he overheard their snide remarks, it was as if the Great Wolf had drawn a sharp claw across his belly.

If it was just him, he wouldn't mind so much, but Graceful . . .

She was sitting alone as usual, he saw, as he looked across the small valley. Self-possessed as she was, he knew she must be lonely. His Mother-Wolf never had been forgiven for taking a dog as her mate, and for giving him pups. Would things have been different,

Pup wondered, if his father had lived? Would they treat Graceful with more respect? Would they even, perhaps, have accepted her half-blood offspring more easily?

Probably not. He sighed, still eyeing Graceful, and padded on. He was jolted out of his reverie when something collided with his shoulder.

"Watch it!" a young wolf snapped, her fangs grazing his neck.

Pup started. He'd walked right into a small gang of his Packmates, and he'd accidentally shouldered Daring, of all wolves. She had a vicious temper at the best of times.

"Sorry—" he began.

"So you should be, runt." Strident curled his muzzle and growled. "Why can't you look where you're going?"

"It was an accident," snarled Pup. "Now let me through."

"Ha." Daring hunched her shoulders and stalked around him, stiff-legged. "You don't tell us what to do, runt."

It was too much. Her contempt, and Bold's overheard scorn, made anger flare in Pup's gut. His hackles sprang erect and he faced Daring full on, his lips peeled back and his own teeth showing.

"Back down, runt." Daring barked a laugh. "You can't challenge me when you don't even have a Name."

"Back down yourself," he snarled. "That works both ways." Challenges were only permitted between fully grown wolves—not that he was afraid of Daring. She was only a few moons older than he was. If she wanted to ignore the rules, he was more than willing to fight.

"You lot!" The angry yelp made the young wolves turn as one.

Beta was watching them, his eyes cold and hard. Daring shrank back under his stare.

"What do you think you're doing?" Beta snarled. "Daring, see to Alpha's bedding. Strident, Fleet wants a young wolf to take a message. Get out of my sight! And the rest of you. Go!" As the wolves bounded hastily away, he snapped, "Not you, Pup."

Pup couldn't help crouching lower as Beta glared at him. For long moments the Pack's second in command was silent; then he curled his muzzle back from his teeth.

"After moonrise tonight," he growled, "you can be beaten in any challenge you choose. But not before. Do I make myself clear?"

Pup dipped his head, but this time it was as much to hide his anger as to show submission. So even his Beta thought he was destined for nothing better than Omega status?

I'll show them all, Pup thought grimly. *I'll prove my blood runs as fierce and strong as any of theirs.*

As soon as he had his Name, he'd challenge Daring—and he'd thrash her, in fair combat. And then? He'd fight his way up the hierarchy, one wolf at a time. He'd climb the ranks till nobody dared treat him—or his Mother-Wolf—with disrespect.

I'll never be any wolf's Omega. Pup looked to the place where the moon would rise, and swore it to the Great Wolf himself.

Never.

CHAPTER TWO

Pup's gnawing anger stayed with him all the way to the den he shared with Graceful, but as soon as he slunk into its familiar warmth, his spirits lightened.

"Hello, Quick," he growled.

His half brother cocked his head and gave him his usual sardonic wolf grin. "Hey, Pup. Soon to be Not-Pup."

Most of Graceful's first litter thought Pup was as far beneath them as the river in the canyon. Pup knew they had never forgiven her for taking another mate—a *dog!*—after their own father was killed in a battle with the Far-Cliff Pack. Quick was different, though. He still came to visit Graceful and he didn't wear a permanent sneer around her lone half-blood offspring.

What was more, thought Pup, he was fun to be around. Quick was named as much for his wit as for his speed in the chase. His remarks could be a bit too smart, but at least he wasn't mean or scornful.

Quick let his tongue hang out. "Now that you're going to get your Name, you can start sending your enemies to the Great Wolf's caverns. Who's going to be first, Pup?"

"Daring," growled Pup, his hackles rising.

"He won't be sending any wolf," said Graceful calmly, licking at a paw. "That's not the point of a Name, Quick. Behave yourself."

"If I behaved myself, Mother-Wolf, I'd never have any fun." Quick nibbled the tip of her ear affectionately. "Hadn't we better get going? There's a fat deer leg I've got my eye on, and I don't want to miss it."

That was Quick, thought Pup: always thinking about his belly. But his half brother was as patient as any of the Pack when the wolves gathered later that evening to share the prey. No wolf would dare eat out of turn, not under the keen eye of Alpha. A powerful pale-coated wolf, she lay on a high slab of rock, holding a haunch of elk down with one huge paw as she gnawed, one yellow eye always on her Pack.

Particularly, tonight, on Pup.

Only when the Pack had eaten and the moon had risen, swollen and silver and high above the tree-spiked horizon, did the wolves gather for the Howl. Pup loved these moments beneath the night sky, when the Great Wolf ran through their dreams, but tonight he found it hard to concentrate. His belly was tight with nerves; the prey was plentiful, but he'd barely been able to gulp down half a rabbit. Perhaps that was why, as wolf voices swelled around him and melded into one great cry, his howl did not seem to quite fit with the others'.

Pup shook himself and tried again, striving to match his pitch to Quick's beside him. His voice was never as strong and as pure as the other wolves', but that was only because of his youth. Wasn't it?

He'd heard the others talk sometimes of how, during the Howl, they would feel the Great Wolf lope down from the stars to walk among them. How she would listen, and answer, and give help to wolves she favored, wolves who had the courage to ask it of her.

Pup squeezed his eyes tight shut. *Great Wolf,* he thought, *give me your blessing. Make me a true Wolf. Make me a part of this Pack.*

However hard he thought it, however loud he howled, he heard no reply. Inside his skull there was only the echo of his own cry. Blinking one eye open, Pup risked a look around the Pack. Their uplifted faces were fierce and joyful, as if every one of them had the Great Wolf howling at their side.

He did not have time to crush down the jealousy that rose in his throat. As the Howl died around him, Alpha gave a ringing bark.

"Come forward, Pup, son of Graceful."

His legs trembled as he rose and paced to the center of the circle. Yellow eyes followed his every move. *I mustn't look afraid.*

"You have come of age, Pup, and now you join our Pack as a true wolf." With a few sharp rips of her fangs and claws, Alpha tore open the belly of Graceful's white rabbit, then flayed it of its skin. Laying her paw on the bloody white pelt, she waited till Pup came forward to sit on it. Then she raised her head again.

"Wolves of my Pack. Name this Pup for his qualities."

Pup swallowed hard. He'd seen this ceremony many times now, and a thrill always ran through his spine when the wolves called out the names they thought would fit the candidate. Sometimes they quarreled over which was best; sometimes a name just seemed to slide over a wolf like a second pelt, and then it was easy and fast. *What will they suggest for me?*

He waited in the silence. No wolf spoke.

Pup swallowed again. He looked around the Pack, desperate to hear a name called, *any* name. Still there was no sound but the gentle sigh of the wind in the pines.

His blood ran hot, then icy cold. *Please . . . one of you . . . name me.*

His eye caught Graceful's. There was shock in her expression. She turned her head to stare at each wolf. Wolf-mothers and sires were not permitted to name their own pups, so she could say nothing herself, but she looked devastated that no other wolf would speak up.

Just when Pup thought the silence might stretch till it snapped, he saw Graceful nudge Quick, hard, with her shoulder. His half brother blinked in surprise, and his friends around him shot him mocking, expectant looks.

Quick. Please, say something. Please.

The young wolf's jaws opened, and he licked his lips, glancing from left to right. He seemed surprised that it had fallen to him.

Quick, you know me! Pup's heart lifted, and the shame of the crushing silence began to slip away. Quick would think of something fine; Quick knew he was a good hunter, that he was strong and fast and brave. Quick would come to his rescue, and then this would be over . . .

Quick drew in a breath, licked his chops again, and gave a sharp, laughing bark.

"DOG."

For an instant the scene seemed to freeze before Pup's eyes. Then the howls rose around him again, but this time they were howls of laughter. Daring was yelping with helpless hilarity, and one of Quick's friends rolled onto his back, unable to contain his hysteria. Even the older wolves were barking with amusement.

"*Dog!*"

"Quick, you devil wolf, that's perfect!"

"Yes! His name is Dog!"

"Quick has spoken!"

"Dog! Dog! Dog!"

Pup suddenly felt life return to his paws, in a wave of helpless anger. He spun on the pelt and faced Alpha.

"Alpha, no! *I am no dog.*"

Slowly, the magnificent she-wolf shook her head. As the howls of laughter began to subside, she gazed at Pup, her yellow eyes unreadable.

"The Pack has spoken," she said. "You are Dog now."

Pup sat motionless on the white pelt, his muscles rigid with the effort of not trembling, as the Pack began to disperse around him. He could still hear their muttering voices, their strangled yelps of amusement.

"Dog!"

"He's called Dog. . . ."

"Was ever a Name more fitting?"

The white rabbit fur beneath him, gleaming in the moonlight, seemed like a stupid practical joke. Glancing down, Pup could see its empty eye sockets, and even those seemed to mock him.

Dog! Ha! I died so they could call you Dog!

Pup slammed his paw down onto the head of the fur, ripping it with his claws. Then he jerked his head high again.

Quick was still sitting there, next to Graceful, whose face was taut with pain and shame. Pup—*no, I'm Dog now, thanks to him*— bounded across to his half brother, drawing his lips back from his fangs and glaring into his eyes, nose-to-nose. Quick flinched just a little, surprised.

"How could you?" snarled Dog. "You're my brother. How could you *betray me?*"

"Betray you? What?" Quick's eyes opened wide and he took a hasty pace back. "Look, calm down, Pu—Dog. I said the first thing that came into my head. That's what you're supposed to do."

"You called me Dog! I have to carry that Name till I go to the Great Wolf!"

"Sky-Pack help us, it's just a Name! Somebody had to say something." Quick hunched his shoulders. "Anyway, it's true. I'm not your brother; can't be. You're not a real wolf. Your father wasn't a wolf *at all*."

Dog felt as if the air had been struck from his lungs. Graceful gave Quick a sidelong look, one full of hurt, and turned back to Dog.

"You have a Name now," she said quietly. "And there's no shame in it." Turning on her haunches, she paced away, her head and tail low.

"Does nothing matter to you?" growled Dog, his saliva spattering Quick's jaw. "Does no *wolf* matter?"

Quick's face hardened and he shook himself. "I care about food and my friends and my Pack. I gave you a Name, didn't I? You should be grateful somebody spoke up. Don't take yourself so seriously." With a flick of his bushy tail, Quick bounded away to rejoin the other young wolves.

Dog stood for long moments in the silver moonlight. It no longer shone on the rabbit pelt, which lay there discarded and crumpled and dirty gray.

One thing was certain, Dog realized. The ceremony had done its job. He was no longer a pup; he'd become an adult in the space of an agonizing heartbeat.

I'm more a grown wolf than Quick. I feel a hundred moons older than him. Dog's muzzle curled.

I'm right: Quick cares about nothing and no wolf. He felt like he was seeing his half brother clearly for the first time. Quick was a joker: funny and lighthearted, fast mouthed and empty headed. Consequences never entered his skull.

Dog was an adult wolf now. He was a full member of this Pack, and that meant he'd be on patrol duty this very night. He was at the bottom of the heap, ranking above only the frail, ancient Omega, but that would not be for long.

I'll watch over the Pack that despises me, he thought. *I'll protect them because it's my duty, and I respect my Pack despite everything.*

And he would claw his way up over their heads, biting the grins off their faces as he went. He'd show them what a Dog could do. He'd prove to them, with his claws and his teeth and his guts, what a Dog could *be*.

CHAPTER THREE

The snows melted from the pine branches and from the ground beneath the Pack's paws, thawing into a warm and fertile Long Light: months when their bellies were full, their coats were sleek, and new pups rolled and squealed in the green grass. Then the trees turned red and gold, and once more the ground froze underpaw, and the snows came again, smothering the landscape in white. But the Pack was strong and the wolves endured the cold well.

Only the weakest of the wolves died that Ice Wind, and Dog was one of the strongest. By the time Long Light warmed the land once more, bringing greenness and wildflowers and the migrating herds, he was a fully grown, powerful wolf; by Red Leaf he was the leader of his own hunting team.

The sun striped his back fur with warm gold as he prowled through the undergrowth, scenting for the mule deer he knew had passed this way. He flicked his ears to scatter the flies that danced around his head, but it was impossible to discourage them. Ignoring their insistent high-pitched whining, he focused all his senses on his prey and on his team.

Off to his left, Noble stalked through the scrub. She'd played with his Mother-Wolf as a pup, and she had plenty of experience and skill. Several wolf-strides from his right flank were Daring and Brave, spread out as he'd instructed. Brave was young, but he was keen. Daring was . . . well, she was as she'd always been, but at least she was a reliable hunter.

Dog paused on the edge of the forest clearing. The buck's head was up, sniffing the wind, but it was blowing toward the wolves. It had a group of four or five does as well as some calves that must have been born in an earlier season; the filtered sun burnished their sleek coats with orange. Any one of them would make a fine catch. *There are four of us*, thought Dog with a surge of hunting-thrill. *How many can we take?*

He flicked an ear toward Noble and glanced at the buck. Turning to Daring and Brave, he indicated the does. Noble gave him a brief nod, but Daring whispered something to Brave, and Dog's brow furrowed.

Dog lowered his forequarters and slunk closer. Their positions were perfect—

There was a crashing of undergrowth to his right as Daring and Brave charged across him toward the buck. It spun in alarm, and the does and the calves bolted for the deeper forest, tails flashing white.

The buck was trying to flee, too, but Daring's claws were already raking its red haunches. With a bellow it turned, lashing its antlers at the two wolves. Dog dashed to help them, even as fury burned in his gut.

I am the leader of this team! What did those two think they were doing? He'd beaten them both—and soundly—to rise above them in the Pack hierarchy, just as he'd challenged and thrashed so many other wolves. He'd left that scar on Daring's shoulder himself!

"Get after those does!" he barked at Noble. "You might still get a calf."

She gave a quick nod and tore into the woods after the deer, but Dog held out little hope; the prey had too much of a head start. Daring and Brave were lunging at the buck's flanks, and Brave even snapped at its head, but that was a bad move—the buck swung its antlers, nearly goring his belly. Daring slashed her claws down its shoulder and Dog leaped to rake its haunches. The creature was still kicking and struggling as Dog grabbed the soft underside of its neck in his jaws. By the time Noble returned, preyless, the stag was on its knees, exhausted from blood loss, and all she had to do was help them finish it off.

As soon as the light died in the buck's eyes and its head flopped to the earth, Dog sprang back, barking furiously at Daring and Brave. "How dare you ignore my orders?"

Daring hunched her shoulders, giving him a sly look. "You told us to attack the buck, didn't you?"

"I told you to go for the does, and you know it!" he snarled. "We could have had two of these deer!"

"We only got this one," she growled, "thanks to me and Brave."

"Really?" He was breathing heavily, and he fought to control his temper. "Since it's your kill, then, you can drag it back to camp. Both of you!"

"Oh, I don't think so." Daring sat back on her haunches and scratched her ear. "Longpaws use dogs for fetching and carrying, so that's your job. Go on, *fetch*!"

The insolence almost knocked the breath from Dog's lungs. He drew himself up, his long legs stiff, his eyes blazing. "*I challenge you.*"

The wolves faced each other for a long, silent moment. Daring got to her paws, but Noble took a sidelong step between them.

"Dog," she said gently, "you're already Daring's superior. You've nothing to *gain*, and everything to lose."

"This isn't about gaining or losing," snarled Dog. "This is about honor. She's not going to get away with that talk. She'll accept my challenge, or I'll make sure she's branded a coward."

He glared into Daring's eyes, glad to see that she blinked first. Of course Daring knew that she would lose to Dog in any fair fight. He'd proved that before, and with ease. Her ears betrayed her with a nervous twitch.

Brave's voice cut into the tension between them. "What challenge? I didn't hear any challenge."

Dog turned to him, his lip curling. "What?"

"No wolf's issued a challenge." Brave tilted his head, and his jaw twisted in a smirk.

"That's right." Daring, her composure back, gave a yelp of amusement. "No challenge here."

"It's our word against yours," sniped Brave.

"And who's going to take a dog's word over a wolf's?" Daring growled. "Let's ask the Pack when we get back, shall we?"

Dog's hackles sprang erect as he stared at them both in disbelief. Swinging his head, he looked at Noble. She was staring at the ground, apparently fascinated by the carpet of pine needles. With a bark of laughter, Daring turned and stalked away, Brave at her heels.

"Don't forget the buck," she called back, her voice brimming with insolence, and then the two young wolves were gone.

Dog shivered with rage beneath his fur. His blood ran hot, and his bones trembled, but there was nothing he could do. He turned to the corpse of the buck and snapped his teeth into its throat.

"I'll help." Noble's small voice was at his ear, and her teeth gripped the buck's shoulder.

Dog released his grip. "Leave it!" he snarled, twisting to glare at her. "I'm the dog. I'll carry the prey."

"You know that isn't—"

"Noble? They called you *Noble*? That's a joke," he growled. "You heard what I said, and what they said, and you kept your jaws shut. *Noble,* hah!"

The older wolf took a pace back, lowering her head. Then she lifted it, and looked sorrowfully into his angry eyes.

"A Name isn't everything, Dog," she said softly. "You of all wolves should know that."

She turned and padded slowly back toward the camp.

* * *

The anger wouldn't shift from his belly. Dog lay in his den, tearing with his fangs at a stout branch pinned beneath his paws. It splintered, spiking into his gums, but he ripped again, furiously, shredding it. The pain was nothing to his churning fury. He had dragged the buck all the way back to the camp by himself. Beta had been disappointed in them for only catching one deer, and Dog knew Beta was right.

"Dog?" said a soft voice behind him.

He glanced sideways, but sank his teeth into the wood again, wrenching it to splinters. *This should be Daring's guts.* "Mother-Wolf," he growled.

"Noble spoke to me. She told me what happened."

"And?" He spat shreds of branch.

"You have to tell Alpha. You *must*. Alpha would want to know about this kind of insubordination. A Pack can't afford to let wolves behave like that. Alpha knows it, she'll take your side, and she'll—"

"That's enough!" Dog sprang to his paws, slamming one of them onto what was left of the wood. "Alpha will hear nothing of this, do you hear me?"

"But Dog—"

"I was the senior hunter!" Dog shoved his muzzle against

Graceful's, and spoke through his clenched fangs. "They were my team, under my command! If Daring thinks she can speak to me that way, it is *my fault.*"

"It was not your fault!" Graceful took a pace back, her gentle eyes wide. "I could explain to Alpha. I could tell her what happened. Dog, this is important—"

"Important? To let every wolf in the Pack know what a pathetic leader I am?" He gave a vicious snarl. "I don't need my Mother-Wolf running to Alpha to tell her all the other wolves are being *mean* to me!"

Graceful's forequarters sagged. "I only want to help."

"Help?" he howled. "You've done enough!"

Graceful caught her breath, and her brow furrowed with confusion. "What do you mean?"

"What went through your head? Go on, tell me!" Dog raked his claws furiously through the soft floor of the cave, drawing a score like a wound. "Didn't you even think twice before you inflicted this on your own pup? What kind of madness got into your brain? You're a wolf, and you mated with a filthy *dog*!"

Graceful stared at him, shaking her head as she backed away, and pain knotted his belly at the expression on her face. For an instant, the anger inside him died, like a forest fire swamped by rain.

She set her jaw, her eyes dark with hurt. "Dog, don't. Don't talk about your sire that way!"

Dog gathered his anger. "You're the one who made him my sire. Not me!"

Fury lit her eyes, and they flashed gold in the dimness. "Don't you dare! Your sire was a fine dog, a strong and a wise dog. Yes, he was a dog, and he was better than a hundred wolves I've known! You should be proud to wear that Name, yet all you can do is listen to vicious fools like Daring. Well, I don't have to. And I don't have to listen to you insult your sire!"

Turning on her haunches, she bounded from the den. Dog stared after her, his insides twisting and tightening with conflicted fury. *How could I . . .*

Graceful's right.

But I'm right too! I can't live like this.

She should never have made me!

With a howl of intolerable fury, he tore the remains of the branch to shreds.

CHAPTER FOUR

The plenty of Long Light never lasted forever, and the longpaws came as the trees turned golden. The deer grew warier even as they dwindled in number, because the longpaws hunted with a ruthless efficiency. Dog had watched them once, from a dense copse of sagebrush, and they had no need to harry a buck, to dodge its antlers and claw at its flanks till the blood ran out of it. They raised strange weapons to their shoulders, loud stick-shaped weapons that spat death, and the deer died without a struggle.

And so the deer were moving on. Yesterday's find had been lucky, too lucky to waste as Daring and Brave had. The wolves were being forced to travel much farther than usual from their snug and secure valley. Although it meant hunger nipped more insistently at their bellies, Dog was glad of the scarcity in one way: It made him even more important to the Pack. His hunting skills were needed like never before.

The morning after Dog's argument with Graceful, they headed down the flank of a narrow valley. Dog was not the leader; his half brother Quick was the one in charge of this team. Brave was loping through the aspens above him, but Daring wasn't with them this time, and Dog was grateful. Here on the far edge of their territory every one of the hunters was uneasy. No wolf wanted a huntingmate they couldn't trust.

The land was much flatter than it was near camp, and looked to Dog as if it had been beaten into submission by the longpaws. Neatly planted corn and grassland extended as far as he could see, hemmed in by longpaws' fences. Sharp, unfamiliar scents stung his nostrils, and he felt horribly on edge. This, he couldn't help thinking, was no place for wolves.

It didn't seem to deter Quick. His brother was digging hard with his claws beneath one of the wooden fences, making a hole big enough for a wolf to wriggle through. Dog could understand that, though, because the scents beyond the fence were far more enticing than any plant smell. The teasing odor in his nostrils was almost like deer, but different. It smelled heavy and warm and meaty and *slow*. One after another, the wolves followed Quick beneath the fence.

"To me, hunters," growled Quick, very quietly, and they

gathered around him, forequarters low and hackles high. "Listen. There's easy prey here, but we have to move in and out fast. The longpaw keeps sheep, and they're guarded only by one old dog, but the longpaw himself has a loudstick."

Shivers of apprehension ran through the hides of the hunters. "Those can kill at a distance," said Dog. "I've seen them."

"And that's why we have to be fast." Quick turned and trotted with long paces into the field, jerking his head to position the other hunters.

Dog was only a few strides from Quick's left flank, and he obeyed his leader—*as any wolf should,* he thought grimly—but the closer they came to the sheep, the greater the uneasiness in his belly. As Quick slowed his pace and flared his nostrils, stalking closer to the oblivious, fluffy white creatures, Dog halted and growled.

"I smell something else, Quick."

"A longpaw? The sheepdog?" Quick's fangs were bared as he licked his chops hungrily. "We'll get out faster if you're quiet."

"It's neither. It's like . . . other wolves," insisted Dog. "Can't you smell them?"

"No! I said, *quiet.* Now!" Quick launched himself at the nearest sheep.

The creature was hopelessly slow and clumsy, its thin legs stumbling beneath its stocky, fleecy body as it bellowed and tried to run. The whole flock began running now, awkwardly and all in one direction.

"This will be easy," barked Quick, snapping at the sheep's neck. "They all stay together. Get another one, Brave!"

It did seem easy, thought Dog as he sprinted to help Quick. *Too easy.* The panicked bellowing of the sheep was almost deafening as they clustered and milled, making useless dashes for escape. The hunters were all around them now, stalking and snarling, snapping at the two fattest to cut them off from their companions.

But despite the noise, Dog could hear something else. The pounding of powerful paws, the low, threatening snarls of a creature to be feared—

"Fierce Dogs!" Brave gave a bark of horror, spinning on his haunches.

Dog released his jawful of fleece and turned to face the newcomers. There were four of them. *So much for Quick's "one old dog"!*

"Brave's right," barked Wise. "Fierce Dogs! They're Longpaw Fangs!"

Strong and sleek, their black-and-brown hides burnished and their ears trimmed to sharp, erect points, the Fierce Dogs seemed to be all white savage teeth as they raced across the field.

"*Fangs?*" barked Dog, aghast.

"Longpaw Fangs! The longpaws use them as weapons." Wise was backing off, the sheep abandoned, but it was already too late. The Fierce Dogs were on them, cutting the wolves off from the sheep flock as easily and skilfully as the wolves had separated the sheep.

Dog backed away as one of the Fierce Dogs launched itself at him, and he rolled onto his flank in a desperate effort to dodge its ferocious teeth. Its comrades were a blur of polished black and brown fur, their claws and jaws raking and tearing through the wolves. For all the wolves' discipline and teamwork, they were scattering and panicking before the onslaught.

The Fierce Dogs seemed to know exactly how to divide the hunting party, shattering all the wolves' attempts to form a defensive line. Quick rolled and lunged for a Fierce Dog's belly, but the creature dodged with slick efficiency and lashed out a savage paw, sending him tumbling away from the other wolves. Dog couldn't even go to his half brother's aid; he was faced down by a snarling dog too big for him to pass, its paws planted determinedly on the grass. Its lips curled back right to the gums, displaying terrifyingly long teeth, and it was stalking forward with death in its glinting eyes. Somewhere to his left he could hear Brave's high panicked barks as a Fierce Dog drove him back.

"Retreat!" barked Quick. "Retreat!"

Dog needed no second telling. *This was a mistake!* With a last snarl at the attacking Fierce Dog, he backed and spun, lowering his tail to flee.

Brave and the others were running too, tails tucked between their legs, but Dog suddenly skidded to a stop, snapping his head back. "Where's Quick?"

The others didn't even pause to listen. Brave was already scrabbling back under the fence and Wise had simply leaped the fence in his panic, crashing against the top rail but catching it with his forepaws as he fell back, then scrambling desperately over.

Dog turned, his tail quivering. The Fierce Dogs weren't giving chase. Ignoring the fleeing hunters, they were hunched over a gray figure on the meadow, snapping and tearing.

Dog felt his shoulders stiffen. *Quick!*

He could see blood spattering as the Fierce Dogs tore at his half brother, all their attention on him now that the other wolves had fled in disarray. *They'll rip out his throat!*

Dog bunched his muscles and sprang into a run, back toward Quick. His paws pounded across the level meadow and he didn't even take a breath to bark, so when he slammed into the nearest Fierce Dog, it was taken completely by surprise. It tumbled and he rolled with it, snarling and biting. The others jerked back from Quick, stunned.

Quick's legs flailed as he fought his way back onto all fours, panting, bleeding from deep scratches. There was a light of terror in his eyes.

"Run, Quick!" barked Dog, just as the first Fierce Dog recovered, sprang upright and flung itself at him.

Quick needed no second telling. Bushy tail pinned tightly between his hindquarters, he fled toward the fence. As Dog made to follow, he heard the snarling breath of the Fierce Dogs behind him. They were all focusing on him now, and he felt claws rake his haunches.

Dog staggered. He swerved, recovering, and veered back toward the fence, but the Fierce Dogs were even more organized than he'd expected. Two of them were coming at him on each flank now. Desperation gave him a burst of speed, and he caught Quick's yellow eyes, staring from the other side of the fence. *Quick made it, at least he made it out—*

"Dog, *faster!*" His brother's howl rang in his ears and gave him extra strength, but an instant later it was drowned out by a distant *bang*.

Dog's paws slid sideways as fear clenched his heart. *That was a loudstick!*

The other wolves knew it, too. They were all running away from the fence now, even Quick, dashing for the trees and for safety.

Wait for me, wait!

A massive blow struck him. One of the flanking Fierce Dogs had barreled into him, and he was flung sideways, his balance lost altogether. An instant later he crashed to the ground, landing awkwardly on his flank, and he felt a blinding pain in his skull. A Fierce Dog plunged onto him, fangs bared, holding him down with its big, heavy paws.

He lay, stunned, waiting for the killing bite, but it didn't come. The world had blurred, and the smells of the air and the meadow made no sense. Even the birdsong sounded distorted, and the panting breaths of the Fierce Dogs as they sniffed at him, and the scratch of their claws on the earth.

"Is it wolf or dog?" The voice sounded distant and echoing, even though he felt the hot breath of the dog against his ear.

"He smells like both." The second growl was harsh and rasping. "We should kill him, then."

"No." That was a third voice, one that sounded crisper than the others, and more commanding. "Wait for the Rancher."

The Rancher. A longpaw.

Terror rippled down Dog's spine, but not even that could make his muscles work. Blackness rushed up on him in a great tide, and he could only lie there limp on the grass as it swallowed him.

CHAPTER FIVE

The light hurt his eyes. Dog thought bright hot sunshine was stream-ing onto him, and for a moment, his head full of fog and pain, he didn't understand. *Am I outside my den? Why?*

He blinked; even that small movement hurt. Slowly his eyes adjusted, and he realized the light wasn't so bright after all. It was dim, in fact—sunlight filtered through cracks in wood.

Wood. Not stone. I'm not in my den.

He lay on his side, sprawled on something scratchy, but he wasn't cold. His nose twitched, finding dry dust that made him sneeze. That hurt, too. Managing to lift his head just a little, he saw that there was straw beneath him; it prickled through his fur and caught between his paw pads.

Dog's nostrils flared again, reaching beyond the dusty straw, and his hackles lifted. The scents were strange. There weren't the usual Pack smells of familiar wolves, milk-warm pups, and last night's prey. He couldn't smell sagebrush or juniper or pine resin, only the overwhelming stink of horse and sheep hide, metal, and sawn wood. And worst of all, longpaw. His nostrils were full of the stench: longpaw sweat and skin and fur, and other sickening odors that were altogether strange.

As he twitched his muscles and stretched his limbs, he discovered that he wasn't badly hurt. *Time to go, Dog. Get out of here.*

He rolled onto his belly, crouched flat, and pricked his ears as he glanced around.

He could focus again, his vision clear and sharp. He lay in some kind of longpaw den, full of straw and the odors of strange animals, but a square of light glowed at the far end of it. That was his way out, then. There was a low wooden fence in his way, but that could be leaped. Beyond the opening in the den, Dog could see a hazy blue line of hills in the distance, jagged with trees. Yearning swept through him, a ferocious need to be running free with his Pack.

Dog hunched his shoulders, set his jaw, and sprang for freedom.

Something around his throat jerked him back in midair, then slammed him to the hard floor with a clatter of chain. A jolt of fresh pain shot through his skull and Dog gasped, his eyes swiveling, tongue lolling. For long moments he lay, shocked, sucking for breath.

No!

Dog scrabbled to his paws and pulled once more toward the open landscape, straining all his muscles, but the thing that held him crushed tight around his throat.

Collared! I'm collared!

His Mother-Wolf had told him about these evil things. Long-paw-mischief! Extending his long claws, Dog dug them under the hide strap that was locked around his neck. There was barely space to get two claws in, but he managed, tearing and tugging, trying to bite and snap at it. It was no use. Dog turned, desperate.

The collar was fastened to a thick chain, and the chain was locked to a stout post that stood in the straw. That was the secret, then. Dog bit on the chain, gnawing, but he realized right away that was useless. He could not afford to break his fangs, not when he was held captive among enemies. Turning with a snarl, he attacked the post instead, tearing at it with his teeth. He could break wood; he often did, ripping apart a branch, relieving his feelings about some new insult from a Pack member.

But this wood was different. As his jaws sank into it, they met hard metal that made his gums shudder. He recoiled at the taste inside his mouth, and tried again. *No.* There was metal inside the wood, making it as unyielding as the chain.

A cold flood of panic went through his bones. *This isn't happening. It can't be.*

Something moved in the square of light, the gap that taunted him with freedom and the open sky. Dog blinked and narrowed his eyes. The shadow moved again, and suddenly he could see it clearly: the slender, powerful shape of a Fierce Dog.

Dog's muscles tensed until they were quivering. He pulled back his lips and showed his teeth as the young female stalked forward to the pen, watching him coolly.

If she'd come to taunt him, she'd get a jawful of abuse in reply. They were all so alike, the Fierce Dogs, with their shining coats and their slender muscles, but he was sure he remembered this one from the battle. However young she was, she was also savage and powerful, and he was sure those teeth had sunk into his flank.

"Are you hurt?" she asked.

Dog blinked, and gave a low distrustful growl.

"Well? Do you have any bad wounds?"

Dog gave a snort of contempt, but he glanced back at his right hindleg. "One bite. Otherwise, just scratches. If I hadn't hit my head on that stone, you'd never have brought me down."

She tilted her head, as if she was amused at his ferocious pride. "Of course not. You'd have defeated us all, I'm sure, and flown home with your wolf wings."

Dog glowered. "Why didn't you just kill me?" he snarled.

"I have no idea." She gave a casual flick of her pointed ears. "It was the Rancher who brought you in. He's the one who put the collar on you. And he must have a reason, because the Rancher doesn't keep anything he doesn't have a use for."

Beneath his fur, a shiver ran down Dog's skin. He didn't want to be of use to the Rancher. Was the longpaw planning to eat him?

"Well," said the Fierce Dog, "there's water in your pen." She nodded toward two large metal bowls he hadn't noticed, tucked in the corner of the pen. "And some food. You might as well eat and drink."

"Why would I trust you?" Dog sniffed suspiciously at the strange dry nuggets that smelled a little like meat. His snout moved to the other bowl. That was far less resistible, and there was no hint of a taint in the clear cold water.

Suddenly Dog realized how thirsty he was; his throat ached with it and his gums were sticky. Hesitantly he dipped his jaws to the bowl, and took a few laps. It seemed pure, even if it didn't taste quite like a mountain stream. He lapped at it again, then raised his head, his muzzle dripping. He licked his chops.

The Fierce Dog was sitting back on her haunches now. "What's your name? I assume you've got one. Mine's Calamity."

Dog eyed her, his tongue lashing his jaws again. Already he felt stronger, after a drink. There was no way he was going to tell a strange and hostile Fierce Dog the Name his Pack had given him, the Name that was a snide joke to most of them. This one was a dog herself, and he didn't want to claim any kinship with her, however distant.

"What kind of a name is Calamity?" His voice was edged with scorn, but he knew he was stalling.

Again Calamity's ears flicked dismissively. "It's not any *kind* of a name, it's just a name. My first longpaws gave it to me, when I was at the training farm."

Just a name? What kind of attitude was that? "That doesn't make sense," Dog told her stiffly. "A Name is everything. A Name is what you are."

"All right. Tell me what you are, then." Her expression grew sly. "What's your name?"

"My Name's none of your business."

"That's a *really* funny name."

Dog bristled. "You know what I mean. And I don't have to tell you my Name."

"Suit yourself." Calamity pricked an ear forward, looking thoughtful. "Well, I'm not barking *Noneofyourbusiness* every time I want to call you, so I'll have to give you a name. I'll call you Wolf."

Dog stiffened. For a horrible moment he thought she was mocking him, just as his Pack would. Then he realized: *No. That's what she truly thinks I am.*

He wasn't a true wolf, but Calamity didn't know that—or she didn't care. If he thought about it, it was almost funny.

With a conscious effort, Dog flattened his hackles. "Go ahead," he growled. "Call me what you like. It's not as if I'll be here for long."

Calamity eyed him, her expression a little supercilious. "All right, Wolf."

She got to her four paws and turned toward the open doorway, but she didn't stalk out. She tilted back her head and gave a volley of deep, resonant barks.

For a little while there was no response, and Dog began to be amused at her pointless summons. But she didn't bark again. She just stood there patiently. He'd have expected her tail to flick at the tip, but he saw with astonishment that she didn't have one—only a small stump.

Another shape appeared at the door, this one tall and upright on two legs. Dog froze. *The longpaw. The Rancher.* Despite himself, he felt his tail fall between his hind legs, and his ears lowered with fear.

The Rancher walked forward to the pen and put a long paw on Calamity's head; she glanced up at him trustingly, but he didn't look at her, only at Dog. Trembling, Dog stared back into his eyes. They were crinkled in the longpaw's sun-beaten skin, and there was a sharp intelligent light in them. Dog's hide tightened and his leg muscles shivered. Something about the Rancher told him that escape from this place was not going to be easy.

There was fur on this longpaw's face that was the same color as his own Alpha's, and that made Dog wonder if this was an Alpha longpaw. He certainly seemed to be the Alpha of these Fierce Dogs. He wasn't quick on his feet and he didn't look sleek and muscled, but Calamity was still gazing up at him, submissive, her eyes warm and soft, and when he uttered a strange longpaw word, she tucked her haunches swiftly under her and sat.

The Rancher leaned over the pen fence as Dog shrank back. Craning his furred head, he studied Dog's face and his legs and his flanks. Dog could feel his keen eyes roaming all over him, and it made his hide itch.

Once again the Rancher patted Calamity's head, and growled some unintelligible longpaw words. Calamity gave a soft whine that sounded like agreement. She turned her head to gaze at Dog with, he thought, exactly the same expression as the longpaw.

Dog's haunches were pressed against the wooden wall at the rear of the pen; there was nowhere he could go, no room to back farther away. *If he comes into the pen, what do I do? Attack him? Try to get past, and run for the hills?*

But the Rancher didn't come in. He made one more coughing sound, gave Calamity a final pat on the head, then turned on his heel and walked out.

Dog didn't understand. Was the longpaw going to leave him here, a prisoner? *Why?* Misery and helplessness rose in his rib cage, threatening to choke him. All he could do was tip back his head, and give a great despairing howl.

CHAPTER SIX

The food in the bowl was not like deer or rabbit, and it tasted strange, but by the time the unseen sun went down and the sky dimmed to blue gray, Dog was ravenous. If he was going to give his captors the slip and run far away from here, he knew he had to keep up his strength. So he mouthed a few of the dry nuggets, wrinkling his muzzle with distaste at first; then he found himself crunching them down faster and faster. He'd gulped the whole bowlful before he realized he'd done it.

He was lapping at the water bowl again, the dry meat having given him a raging thirst, when he heard the click of claws on a timber floor. Four dogs, he realized, pricking his ears forward as he drank. Slowly he raised his dripping muzzle.

"That's about all you can hunt, isn't it, Wolf?" The dog in the lead's lips wrinkled back in a sneer. "Food from a sack."

Another of the Fierce Dogs gave a bark of laughter. "No

wonder his Pack abandoned him. He's not much of a wolf at all, is he?"

Dog stared at them, cold with loathing. Calamity was with them, though she said nothing.

"Let me out of this pen," he growled, "and I'll show you what kind of a wolf I am."

"Oh, you'll be out of there soon enough." The leader took a pace forward, sniffing disdainfully at the fence. "You're one of us now. Get used to it."

"I'm not one of you."

"You will be," grunted the second dog. "The Rancher wants it, so that's what will happen."

"That's if you don't want to be put down," added the leader.

Dog narrowed his eyes. "Put where?"

All four of them laughed this time. "Put nowhere, just put down forever! Put down so you'll never get up again!" barked the leader, showing his fangs. "With the loudstick."

A ripple of fear shuddered through Dog's hide.

"So," went on the leader, when Dog did not reply, "we'd better introduce ourselves. I am Sundance, and I'm the Alpha of your new Pack. Don't ever forget it. This is Zorro"—he nodded at his second in command—"and these two are Belle and Calamity."

Dog's eyes caught Calamity's. Hadn't she told them, then, that she'd already been in here talking to him? "Those aren't proper Names, and I don't need to know them. I'm not going to be part of your Pack. My own Pack's coming back for me, with a lot more wolves."

He tried to sound more convinced than he felt, but even so, Sundance's muzzle curled. "No. They're not. You think they'd risk our jaws for a creature like you?"

"Even if they don't I'll get away myself," snapped Dog.

"What incredible teeth you must have," yawned Sundance, sitting back on his haunches. "I look forward to seeing you bite straight through that chain."

There was nothing Dog could say to that. All he could do was snarl in defiance. But at that moment he heard it: a distant, mournful howling that echoed in the faraway blue hills.

Dog's skin shivered beneath his fur, and his muscles went rigid. He stood quite still on all fours, his ears and nostrils and whiskers yearning toward the sound. If he pricked his ears hard enough, he might make out voices he knew—Graceful, perhaps, or Quick. He'd even be glad to hear Daring.

But the Fierce Dogs had heard it, too. They turned, tensing, their hindquarters quivering as they listened to the sound. A very low, constant growl began to rumble in Sundance's throat.

He gave an abrupt commanding bark. "Form up! We're going wolf hunting!"

"No!" barked Dog, but they had already raced from the barn. Straining at his collar, he let out a frantic volley of yelps. Once again he ripped with his claws at the collar, and he turned to tear uselessly with his fangs at the wooden post. It was hopeless.

I'm trapped in this awful place, he thought in agony, *while those dogs attack the wolves who came to rescue me!* Despair and fury surged in his blood, but even that rush of sensation couldn't give him enough strength to break the post. At last, panting, his flanks heaving, he could only stand there, the collar taut around his throat, and stare through the open barn door.

The hills were invisible now except as empty shadows against a star-speckled sky. The blackness of the night felt oppressive, and Dog could no longer hear barks or howls or yelps, even in the far distance.

He lay down, his head on his paws, and waited.

It seemed an achingly long and tense time before moving shadows appeared on the meadow, growing larger as they approached the barn.

Dog's heart sank in his rib cage. It was the Fierce Dogs, back from their hunt, all four of them in one piece.

Sundance stalked into the barn and right up to the pen fence, head high, an expression of arrogance on his face. His eyes flashed with the excitement of a fight. "I love a good chase."

Chase? Not a fight? "They'll be back," growled Dog.

"I doubt that," said Zorro. "They weren't even coming for you this time."

"You're lying." Dog curled his muzzle back from his fangs.

"He isn't," mocked Sundance. "Those flea-bitten brutes you call a Pack weren't on their way here. They were leaving. *Without you.* We made sure they did it a lot faster."

Dog's breath was coming in fast panicked rasps now. "That isn't true. They'll come for me!"

"We've driven them farther into the mountains." Belle cocked her head to watch him with contempt. "They won't be back to raid the Rancher's sheep. We made sure of that, even though they'd have been too frightened anyway."

"Cowards," spat Sundance, licking his shoulder. "And we only had to kill one of them."

Dog's blood ran cold. Somehow he knew Sundance wouldn't lie; why would he bother? "Which wolf did you kill?" Dog's bark was so hoarse he could barely hear it himself.

"How would I know?" Sundance's ears flicked. "Some old she-wolf who couldn't run fast."

"I don't think she couldn't run," remarked Zorro, giving Dog a sly look. "She was dragging behind, that's all. Kept staring back, like she didn't want to leave."

Dog felt incapable of moving, almost incapable of breathing. Zorro was still watching him insolently.

"So it was her own fault Sundance brought her down. Isn't that right, Boss?"

"I had to give a lesson to the others, anyway," growled Sundance. "And she didn't even bother to beg. Just kept asking what had happened to her pup. The one who got left behind at the longpaw's ranch." Zorro smirked.

"Don't worry. I told her you were fine." Sundance bent to lick idly at his paw. "I told her you'd begged to join the Fierce Dogs. Told her you'd rolled over and pleaded to be in our Pack." He raised his head to stare at Dog. "So I'm sure she was perfectly content when I killed her."

Dog flew at him. Barking, raging, howling, he flung himself again and again at the Fierce Dogs, scrabbling wildly in hopeless fury. The collar jerked so tight around his throat it dug into his flesh with every lunge, and he was gasping for breath, but still he threw himself forward. His vision was blurred and red, darkening by the instant.

It was useless. As the fury drained from his veins, he staggered, then lurched sideways, collapsing to the timber floor. His tongue lolled as he dragged breath into his lungs, the collar almost strangling him. Before his dulling vision he saw the shapes of three Fierce Dogs turn contemptuously and pace out of the barn.

"Wolf. Wolf!" Calamity was still there. She was lying on her forepaws, her nose stretched out through the wooden railings. "Wolf, you have to calm down."

"Calm down?" He lurched to his paws again, struggling. "No!"

"Yes, Wolf. Stop fighting. Please, you'll hurt yourself."

"Hurt? He killed my Mother-Wolf!" His strangled barking hoarsened as he felt the collar tighten again.

"Don't let him do the same to you!" Calamity stood up, pressing her face to the bars of the fence.

Flanks heaving, Dog stared at her, still gasping for breath. He backed off a pace, and felt the collar loosen a little. His throat was a dry agony.

"They left you." There was anger in Calamity's voice, but Dog had the odd feeling she wasn't angry with him. "Don't give

Sundance the satisfaction of choking yourself, because your Pack isn't worth it. They've abandoned you."

It's true. They've gone to the mountains without me.

"Quick will come," he whined, but he didn't even believe it himself now.

"Quick, whoever he is, has turned tail and fled. He's left you here with the Rancher and with us." Calamity's words were harsh, but her voice was gentle.

Quick was never going to come for me. He truly doesn't care and he never has.

Dog tipped his head back and let out a ringing, grief-stricken howl. *Graceful is dead. She's dead.*

He would never speak to her again, would never curl up against her warm flanks in their den. She would never lie quietly, telling him stories of his lost sire, reassuring him that his Name was a fine one, a Name to be proud of. *Graceful's dead, and she thinks I abandoned her with a happy heart.*

He'd left her with harsh words. He'd never told Graceful he was sorry for what he'd said about his sire, sorry for the shame he felt about his blood. *And now I never will.* His howl rose in pitch, echoing with remorse and regret. He wished it could reach Graceful, running now with the Great Wolf, but he knew no howl, however piercing, could do that.

I've lost her forever.

As Dog lay down on his forepaws, sunk in his misery, Calamity turned and paced sadly from the barn, leaving him alone to grieve.

CHAPTER SEVEN

Through a dark fog of sleep and grim dreams, Dog heard a sharp clatter that made his head jerk up from sleep. Dizzied, he blinked at the morning sunshine that slanted into the barn, burnishing the straw with early golden light.

Dog kicked out, raking the straw beneath him as he staggered to his paws. The Rancher was there, right in the pen with him, setting down fresh bowls of water and dusty dry meat.

Dog hunched his shoulders low, a growl beginning at the back of his aching throat. This was the longpaw who had taken him from his Pack, had sent his Fangs to kill Dog's mother. Dog sprang at him.

The fur-faced longpaw turned with surprising agility. Too late Dog saw the hefty stick in his hand; he felt it smack down across his muzzle.

Flinching back, Dog was unable to suppress a shocked

whimper of pain. The Rancher was eyeing him closely but without fear. His long-fingered paws were sheathed in thick hide and he held the stick in both of them, alert and ready to whack it down again.

Dog's eyes shifted to the bowl of food; the Rancher was between it and him. If he couldn't even eat—

He lunged again, his fangs bared. Once more the stick smacked down, catching his skull hard enough to make stars explode behind his eyes. Dog whined and shrank back.

This is intolerable! Dog snarled and jumped, and this time the stick caught him on the nose again, even harder. He yelped and crouched, confused and angry.

The Rancher only watched him, tapping the stick lightly against one of his sheathed paws. Dog eyed him back, wary now and afraid of that stinging stick. He took a couple of shuffling paces forward toward the food bowl, his stomach growling and his jaws slavering with hunger. When the Rancher didn't hit him again, he crawled past his feet, almost close enough to touch the longpaw. He pulled himself up, dipped his muzzle into the bowl and began, resentfully, to eat.

The Rancher's front paws were so nimble, Dog's mouth was still full of meat nuggets when he felt the pressure on his neck ease. The longpaw had loosed him from the wooden post! For a moment he was too confused even to swallow, and then he felt a new and different pressure on his throat.

Another collar. Different!

This one felt cold, like metal instead of hide, with a stiff leash already attached to it, tethering Dog to the Rancher's paws. Dog turned, snapping, but the collar instantly contracted on his throat. He went rigid, his eyes rolling. Only when he let his muscles relax did the collar loosen too, and he could breathe easily again.

"Wolf." The voice was familiar.

He looked around. Calamity stood outside the pen with the other Fierce Dogs, watching every move the Rancher made.

"The Rancher is your Alpha now, Wolf," she told him. "Just accept that, and do as he tells you. The sooner you learn it, the sooner the collar will stop squeezing you."

Dog tucked his tail tightly between his hind legs. He couldn't help it—the squeeze collar frightened him. When the Rancher twitched on its stiff leash and nudged him toward the pen's open gate, Dog wanted to resist, but the thought of the collar forced him to obey. He slunk after the longpaw, his hackles rigid with fear.

Despite the Rancher and the squeeze collar and the Fierce

Dogs around him, it was bliss for Dog to step outside the dusty barn and into the cool sunlit air. The sky was blue enough to hurt his eyes, and off in the distance the tree-edged hills were hazy. His nostrils twitched, finding the heavy warm scent of sheep that had got him into this trouble in the first place. Despite that, their meaty odor was irresistible, and Dog jerked toward the milling creatures in a corner of the meadow. Instantly the squeeze collar tightened, and he gasped a wheezing breath. Shivering, he shrank back.

"Now." Sundance padded around the Rancher to gaze at Dog with disdain. "We'll begin your training."

Dog had no intention of being trained, but every day for a full change of the moon the Rancher would come to his pen and bring him out into the field. The squeeze collar and the snapping jaws of the Fierce Dogs were always with him, and the Rancher's loud-stick was never far from his thoughts.

By the end of Dog's first day of training, he had grown to hate the squeeze collar with a fierce passion. The Rancher would not let him make so much as a move without a sharp bark of command, and if Dog rebelled, the metal would tighten on his soft throat muscles. Dog didn't want to do anything this cold-voiced longpaw told him to do. By the time the sun went down and Dog was tethered back to the wood-and-metal post, his jaws were flecked with foam and his throat stung from the collar and from thirst.

Each time the Rancher barked an order, Sundance, at his side, would snap an instruction at Dog, letting him know what the longpaw wanted. At least he could understand the Fierce Dog's commands, thought Dog angrily. At least then he could obey whatever pointless command the longpaw gave, and the collar would leave him alone.

At every hesitation, at every sullen growl, the collar would tighten again. By the middle of the second day Dog had begun to obey swiftly, if only so that he wouldn't choke to death. Some words the longpaw snapped so often, after a few days Dog began to recognize them. By the time the moon had turned from full and round to a bright sliver in the sky, he knew how to respond to them. He felt an odd sense of achievement at no longer needing the scornful Sundance to interpret his Alpha's barks. If the Fierce Dogs were smart enough to understand the Rancher, Dog could learn to do it too. *Heel* was easy enough: walk beside the Rancher. *Sit* sent him back on his haunches. *No:* well, that clearly meant *Stop what you're doing or the collar will tighten.*

And if he was unsure, then the responses of the other Fierce Dogs gave him a clue. It was obvious to Dog that they really did see the Rancher as their Alpha. At the first sound of his voice, each dog would leap to obey, and when they'd done what he asked, he gave them something fine-smelling from a pouch at his side. Dog watched that behavior, licking his chops, but he wouldn't beg. *I won't take his stinking rewards. I hate him, and I hate his Fangs.*

And yet . . . he had nowhere else to go. Every now and then the knowledge would pierce him, making his belly twist with regret and sorrow. *My Pack has left me; what choice do I have? Where else can I go?*

And it was strange, but somewhere deep in his bones he began to feel a tug at the sound of the Rancher's voice. He struggled against the urge to respond, desperately trying to resist, to remind himself that he was a wild wolf . . . but without disobeying so that the Rancher would use the squeeze collar or give him another sharp tap across the muzzle with his stick.

There was something else, too: He was beginning to admire these Fierce Dogs' pack behavior. They moved as if they were a single creature, a single mind. They worked as a team, with all the discipline his Pack had lacked, the strength of trusting teamwork that would have served them so well in a hunt. The realization struck him at the end of a long day of *sit*, *heel*, and *fetch*, as he watched the Fierce Dogs fan out across the meadow to chase the sheep into their dens for the night. Not one of them broke the perfect line that swept across the grass or tried to sneak a bite of the sheep for themselves.

These dogs would never abandon a Packmate. Not ever.

The thought itched at his mind as the days wore on. How many days had it been since he'd been abandoned here? Fifteen, twenty? He had lost count, though he knew the moon had vanished and returned again as it always did.

His misery at his Pack's desertion was warming slowly to anger. In a way he was glad of the relentless training, the hard repetitive work the Rancher was putting him through, because he had no time to gnaw endlessly at what his Pack had done to him. It was there, in the corner of his mind, that was all, niggling and distracting, but the rage couldn't eat at his guts. There was too much to do, and it was becoming instinctive.

By the time the moon was a shining circle in the sky once more, Dog barely remembered a time when he didn't wake up with the scent of sawn wood, the fuzzy coats of the sheep, and the bowl of satisfying dry food. When he followed the longpaw out into the meadow for his training, it was as if they'd been working together for many moons instead of just one. The Rancher gave a command, and Dog's body obeyed it.

Obeyed! The realization almost brought him to a halt as he walked at the Rancher's command; but his legs moved anyway, keeping to the longpaw's side. The strange urge in his bones, the yearning to listen, had taken over command of his muscles. And he hadn't even paused to cock his ear to the Rancher's words.

"*Sit.*" The word brought his haunches beneath him, his tail tucked close, and he looked up at the Rancher.

The Rancher's face wrinkled, an expression Dog had learned went with the patting and scratching gestures that the Fierce Dogs seemed to enjoy so much. The longpaw rummaged in that sweet-smelling pouch. Dog took the small chunk of dry pig meat he offered, gulping it down. It tasted every bit as good as it had smelled when the others were rewarded.

The longpaw leaned over him, so close Dog could have snapped at his furred throat, but the urge seemed to have abandoned him as thoroughly as his Pack had. The Rancher's paws were at his throat, taking off the squeeze collar and fitting another.

The longpaw straightened, and he gestured at the far side of the field. "*Rope. Fetch.*"

Dog knew both words now. It didn't even occur to him to question the Rancher's command; he bounded across the field, loving the freedom of the new collar and the feel of the mead-owgrass beneath his racing paw pads. As his jaws closed on the coil of rope by the paddock fence, he glanced up and felt a rush of pleasure to see Calamity at his side. Her jaws were parted happily and her ears were pricked forward.

"You're doing a brilliant job, Wolf."

He panted for a moment, unsure how to answer. Calamity gave him a low bark of encouragement.

"Keep it up, and you'll sleep in a proper dog bed tonight with us. Your new Pack! It's warm and cozy, Wolf. Wouldn't that be wonderful?"

Slowly, he found himself nodding. "I suppose it would . . ."

I'd like that, he thought. *I'd like not to be cold and alone in the barn. I'd like to have treats from the pouch, to eat well, to sleep with a Pack that's confident and strong and disciplined.*

Anyway, he thought: Would it be so bad to be a Longpaw Fang? Would it be so bad to work for the Rancher, to do his bidding and hear his voice praise Dog for a job well done? To be appreciated by a strong Alpha?

I'd like to please the Rancher. The thought made his tail tap with enthusiasm, even as somewhere in his gut it horrified him.

As the sun dipped behind the ranch house, he padded with

the Fierce Dogs at the Rancher's back, tired, his legs aching, but with an odd and not unpleasant sense of work well done. He was led not back to the barn, but to a shed closer to the Rancher's house.

The longpaw fastened a rope to the new, softer collar; it was loose and it gave him more range than the one in the barn. The metal bowl beside him was full of the meat nuggets that seemed much more appealing than they had the first time he'd tried them.

He gulped at them, not caring about the loose rope that tangled between his legs. Sundance growled and snapped, and he and Zorro shoved Dog's head aside so that they could steal some of his food, but there was more than enough, and Dog ignored their sniping. It was more than he'd ever eaten with his traitorous Pack.

"Wolf, you can sleep here," whined Calamity softly, wriggling aside on a big patterned cushion.

"He should sleep in a dirt heap," growled Zorro.

Sundance rumbled in agreement. "Like he did with those filthy wolves."

Dog decided he wouldn't dignify their scorn with any retort, but Calamity snapped, "Shut your jaws, both of you. Wolf worked well today."

Gratefully, Dog settled himself on half of the bed beside her.

It gave under his weight, fitting snugly around him and warming his hide. Even warmer, though, was Calamity's flank, pressed against his. He could feel her muscles twitching as she began to drowse. With the other Fierce Dogs so close, Dog thought he might not be able to relax, but his tiredness and the comfort overwhelmed him. He fell asleep to the sound of Calamity's steady breathing, the rise and fall of her sides, and the scent of her hide in his nostrils.

CHAPTER EIGHT

Against the low line of the mountains, a huge pale moon was rising. The grass and trees shimmered under a silver light that was strong enough to cast Wolf's shadow. Another long shadow stretched beside his: Calamity's. She padded close by his side as Wolf and his new Pack made their way back to the shed from a day's herding work.

"Did you see how Zorro let that ewe play him for a fool?" whispered Calamity.

Wolf glanced over his shoulder. The other three Fierce Dogs walked together, a few paces behind. He knew he'd turned out to be very good at his job, and Sundance and his cronies had never quite forgiven him for it, or Calamity for liking him. Even now Belle was shooting him a filthy look.

"The ewe wasn't even that smart." Wolf grinned. "All she had to do was pin herself in the corner. He didn't have a clue what to do except bark like an idiot."

"He lost his head." Calamity gave a snort of laughter. "And Zorro thinks he's so smart." She gave Wolf a sudden, affectionate lick on the jaw.

Wolf felt a thrill run through his hide. He swept his tongue over her pointed ear in return. As they trotted into the shed, he followed her to the bed and sat, pricking his ears at the Rancher as he waited for him to clip his leash to the wall.

But the Rancher didn't. He settled Sundance and Zorro and Belle, then turned to Wolf and Calamity with a wave of his front paw.

"*Heel.*"

After these last few moons, Wolf didn't even have to think about the response. He was on his paws as fast as Calamity, walking at the Rancher's side as he led them back out of the shed.

"What's happening?" he whispered past the Rancher's striding legs.

Calamity looked happy, her eyes shining. "It's our turn to stand guard tonight. That means our Alpha completely trusts you!"

Wolf felt his heart swell, and not only with pleasure at his Alpha's confidence in him. He remembered his nights of patrol duty with his old Pack, before he was promoted to be a hunter. Those nights had been long and usually boring, since his fellow Packmates would barely exchange a civil word with him. He'd never had such pleasant company as Calamity.

The Rancher stopped, patting their heads and offering each of them a treat from the pouch before striding off toward his home. Wolf and Calamity were about to set off along the fence when a shadow moved behind them.

"Calamity," growled Sundance.

She tilted her head. "Yes, Sundance?"

"You're in charge." The Fierce Dog shot a glower at Wolf. "You're to make sure the sheep are safe, but you're also to make sure Wolf behaves himself. I don't want any mistakes."

"Oh, don't worry." Calamity rolled her eyes and sighed. "I'll keep a *very* close eye on him." She grinned at Wolf, and let her tongue loll.

Wolf felt a rumble of amusement in his throat, but he managed to repress it while Sundance fixed him with his hostile eyes. Then Calamity was trotting happily off along the fence, and with a last glare at Sundance, Wolf followed.

Just as he'd expected, Calamity was a good patrol companion. Quietly, they paced between the sheep pens and the farmhouse, sniffing and pricking their ears for any sign of trouble. Wolf's fur prickled with alertness, and as the moon rose higher he kept his paws quiet and his nose sensitive to every fleeting scent. But as the time passed, and he detected no threats, he began to relax. With the quiet, intent Calamity at his side, he felt as if they were a single entity, a perfect partnership. Each of them seemed to know without speaking when to pause and sniff, and when to move on. No enemy had a chance of getting past them.

As they halted by the meadow fence, Calamity sat down and tilted her head. "It's so calm. Nothing's even moving. How about a race?"

Wolf's ears came forward. "A race?"

"Yes. Not scared, are you?" She squirmed through the gap between the fence and the gate. "Oh, of course you are. I'm sorry! You know I'll beat you!"

"Ha!" Wolf wriggled through after her. "You'll be sorry you said that!"

"The far fence and back." She sprang into a run, taking him by surprise, and her haunches were already several paces ahead of him when he started after her. Wolf sprinted, his paws pounding, his leg muscles extending his stride until he was abreast of her; then he drew ahead. Beneath his paws the grass was damp and moon-silvered, and he could hear her panting, laughing breaths close behind.

I've never been this happy, he thought, with a sweet sense of shock.

At the fence, Wolf skidded in the earth onto his haunches, twisted and leaped back the other way. Calamity had turned early, taking a sneaky advantage, but still he caught up, flying past her. When they reached the fence, she collided with his hindquarters and they tumbled to the ground in a tangle of legs. Wolf grabbed her neck in his jaws, but gently, play-shaking her until she twisted from his grip and grabbed his muzzle in hers.

At last, exhausted, they flopped together onto their sides, tongues lolling. Above them the stars were brightening despite the hugeness of the moon. Scents of pine and aspen and sagebrush drifted to Wolf's nostrils, but he felt no urge to run to the hills. He wanted to stay right here.

"Calamity," he said, and hesitated.

"What?"

He licked his chops, getting his breath back. *And not just because of the race,* he realized. "I just . . . I don't really know how to say this, but . . . "

"Give it a try." She twisted her head to stare at him.

It came out in a rush. "I've never liked any wolf or dog as much as I like you."

For a moment she was silent, and he thought his heart had stopped beating in his chest.

"I feel that way too," she murmured at last.

A rush of relief and happiness swept through his hide. "Oh. Good."

"Wolf, do you still think about running away?" Her eyes were dark and steady on his.

He cocked an ear toward the hills and sighed. "Yes," he admitted. Then he met her eyes again. "But if you'll be my mate, I'll stay here forever."

Her jaws opened and her eyes widened, but before she could speak again, there was an eruption of panicked squawking across the yard.

"The chicken cages!" Calamity bounded to her paws.

Wolf sprang up and ran. Sure enough, the racket was coming from the wire cages where the fat chickens roosted, and there was a tang in his nostrils that he remembered from his wild days. Not wolf, not fox . . . His lips peeled back from his teeth.

Coyote!

"You take the yard side!" he growled, and Calamity peeled away, running round the wire fencing. Wolf slowed, his legs stiff as he stalked closer to the tall gate. He could see now where the wire hung agape, the catch left carelessly loose. *My territory,* he thought savagely. *And these birds belong to my Alpha. No coyote takes prey from my protector. . . .*

Silently he crept closer, nudging the gate wider, easing his shoulder into the run. *There!*

Wolf stopped, one paw lifted.

Coyotes usually ran in gangs, he knew that, but this one was alone. *Like me. Like I was. . . .*

In the hatched moonlight Wolf could make out the coyote's jutting ribs, its disheveled coat. As it moved stealthily toward the frantically clucking chickens, it lurched oddly, and Wolf realized it was using only three of its skinny legs. He moved along the inside of the cage, watching it, stunned by pity.

Wild thing. Exiled from its Pack. Alone and hungry . . .

The coyote lunged, snatching a red hen. Its eyes widened as it caught sight of Wolf, and then it darted past him, a flash of pale scraggy fur, and shot through the open gate.

No! Wolf twisted and raced after it, but he could already hear the pounding paws of the other Fierce Dogs. They were running across the yard, cutting off the coyote as it fled in panic, the chicken hampering it.

Sundance reached it first, pouncing and slamming the smaller creature to the ground. The coyote rolled and tumbled, dropping the chicken, but by that time Zorro and Belle were on it as well. Teeth snapped and claws flashed, and when the panting Fierce Dogs at last drew back, the coyote was nothing but a bloody scrap, limp and tattered in the mud. The chicken was a lifeless heap of rumpled feathers beside it.

Sundance tipped back his head and raised the alarm, sharp deep barks that Wolf knew would summon the Rancher. His hide and his spine chilled. *What have I done?*

Or what have I failed to do?

As the Rancher came hurrying from the house, a beam of light bouncing in his paw, Sundance spun on his haunches and loosed a ferocious snarling howl right in Wolf's face. Wolf could do nothing but stand rigid, his fur prickling. Even Calamity, padding miserably to his side, couldn't reassure him.

This was my fault. I hesitated too long, showed too much pity. Now they'll separate us. The Rancher will chain me up again.

He backed closer to Calamity as Sundance, Zorro, and Belle surrounded them both. His hackles rose, but he knew there was no point attacking his Packmates. He couldn't fight three.

And Calamity. What about her?

The two of them stood trembling together; Wolf could feel the quivering of her hide. Zorro and Belle lowered their forequarters and snarled as Sundance took another pace forward.

"You've let the Pack down. *You've let down our Alpha!* You've failed, both of you!"

"Sundance," Wolf began. "It was my—"

"*Be silent!* You can't be trusted!" Sundance's vicious head swiveled to Calamity. *"Neither of you!"*

She crouched, trying to lower her pointed ears. "I'm sorry, Sundance."

"You will be. You failed in your most solemn duty. You'll both be punished."

CHAPTER NINE

The barn door slammed behind the Rancher, and he was gone. The fact that he hadn't said a single angry word did not reassure Wolf. He and Calamity pressed against the barn wall, eyeing the three Fierce Dogs who held them pinned there.

Inside the vast barn it was shockingly dark, as if the great moon outside had been extinguished altogether. But Wolf could still make out the glint of hatred in Sundance's eyes. He glanced at Calamity. She was watching her Alpha, and her limbs were shaking, but her eyes did not drop from Sundance's.

For the first time in weeks, Wolf felt the old wild wolf anger rising in his chest. What right did these Fangs of Longpaws have to threaten him? What right did they have to threaten his *mate*?

He took an aggressive pace toward Sundance, turning his body slightly to shield Calamity. "What kind of punishment?" he growled.

"Not as much as you deserve," snarled Sundance. "You'll be marked. Permanently. At least that will remind you to do your duty."

Wolf froze. *Marked? How?* But before he could respond, Zorro and Belle sprang for him, knocking him to the ground and pinning him down with their powerful forequarters. Wolf struggled, snapping and twisting, but there were two Fierce Dogs on him and they were strong.

Sundance moved swiftly. One of Wolf's forelegs sprawled on the floor, and the Fierce Dog lunged, raking his claws down Wolf's paw. For a second Wolf didn't feel it; then the pain hit. He howled. The slash in his flesh was deep and bloody.

Zorro and Belle rolled off him and stood up as Wolf cringed back, licking frantically at his paw. As he rested it on the ground he felt pain shoot up his foreleg again, but he could tell it wasn't so serious as to lame him. He'd still be able to walk and run. Sundance knew exactly what he was doing.

Wolf would carry the shameful scar for life.

They've done this to me for the sake of a chicken. And I let them do it! He raised his head to glare his hatred at Sundance. *If I'd been a real wolf, I'd have taken the hens myself. And I would never have let him do this to me!*

"Calamity," growled Sundance. "Show me your paw."

Wolf's fury drained abruptly, replaced by horror. "No! It was my fault! *Me.* You can't punish her, she didn't—"

"She was your fellow guard, and I warned her she was in charge. It's as much her fault as it is yours. Your paw, Calamity."

With one glance at Wolf, Calamity stepped forward. Zorro and Belle didn't even need to pin her down. She lay down on her belly, her head pressed low, and extended her foreleg toward Sundance.

"No!" barked Wolf, and sprang forward.

Teeth seized the soft skin of his neck, and another set of jaws grabbed his shoulder. Zorro and Belle wrestled him down, not breaking the skin this time, but gripping him hard enough to hurt and dragging him back from Calamity and Sundance. Wolf could do nothing but watch as Sundance raised his paw and slashed Calamity's sleek forepaw.

Wolf heard her give the faintest, choked whine.

Zorro and Belle released him contemptuously, and Wolf staggered, but he couldn't even snap at them. He could only stare at the shivering Calamity as the three other Fierce Dogs stalked disdainfully to the barn door. It opened to Sundance's yelp, and he heard the Rancher's low voice praising the brute before the door closed again.

Calamity half rose and slunk to a pile of straw, turning and curling up. If she'd had a tail, it would have been tucked tightly beneath her legs. She didn't look at Wolf as he padded hesitantly up to her, then gently licked the tip of her ear.

She flinched from his touch. "Leave me alone."

"I'm sorry, Calamity, you didn't deserve this—"

"Yes. I did." Her voice was muffled. "Sundance is right. I failed in my duty."

"You didn't. I did." Stepping close, Wolf tried to settle down beside her, but suddenly she raised her head and snapped.

"I said, leave me alone!"

Wolf backed off, shocked. He tightened his tail between his legs as he stared at the back of Calamity's head. *She blames me. And she's right.*

His heart like a stone of misery in his rib cage, Wolf padded to the barn door and lay down. It wasn't latched or locked; the Rancher knew his dogs would never run away. He was their Alpha, wasn't he?

Wolf nudged open a narrow gap so that he could gaze out at the speckled black sky over the far hills. He only knew where the hills were because that was where the stars stopped.

I pitied that coyote, just for a moment. And look where it got me. Scarred for life, and Calamity too.

Wolf wished that he could sleep, but his mind was in turmoil. *What am I doing here? I'm as pitiable as that coyote, and it's dead.* Sundance, he knew, would have liked to give Wolf the punishment he'd given the coyote. But his scar of shame—was even that a proper punishment for one mistake? What kind of a Pack was this?

But how could I ever live without a Pack?

Rising, he nudged the barn door wider and limped out to the yard. The moon was smaller now, and lower in the sky, but it was still there. Wolf sat back on his haunches and let out a howl of desperate misery.

Great Wolf, help me. Who am I? Dog or Wolf?

As his howl faded, something tingled in his hackles. He went still.

No giant starlit wolf bounded down from the night sky, like she did in the old stories. But he'd felt *something.*

It was like a tug, insistent and demanding, at the nape of his neck. Something was calling him—calling him away from here, away toward the hills. He smelled sagebrush and aspen on the breeze again, and this time he yearned toward it.

The forest. I have to be there. Not here.

And yet . . .

Wolf padded on silent paws back into the barn. Calamity still lay in the straw, absolutely still, but he knew she wasn't asleep. He nudged her muzzle, very gently, with his own.

"Calamity," he whispered. "I need to leave this place."

Slowly she raised her slender head and turned it toward him. Her eyes were dark and very clear, but unhappy. "What about your promise?"

"I still want you to be my mate. But I can't stay here. Come with me. Please, Calamity."

For long moments she gazed at him; then she shook her head.

"This is my family," she whispered. "The Rancher. Sundance and Zorro and Belle. Whatever else they are, they're my Pack."

Wolf took a breath. "Even though they—"

"Yes. Even though they did that. Wolf, I'm happy here. It's the only world I've ever known. I don't belong in yours."

"I think you do." Closing his eyes, he nuzzled her jaw.

"I can't, Wolf. Don't ask me. I can't."

If I leave, then, I leave without Calamity.

"In that case," he murmured, "I'll stay." His heart was heavy inside him, but he knew he couldn't leave her. "I'll stay with you."

"No." Giving a great sigh, she gazed into his eyes. "Wolf, you have to go. You *need* to go."

"But—" Pain sawed inside him.

"If you stay, now? With me? You'll grow to hate me."

"No! I—"

"Yes, you will. You'll hate me for keeping you here and you'll hate yourself for letting me." She licked his face gently. "You're right, Wolf. You can't be happy here. So go, right now. I'll give you as much of a start as I can. I promise. But I'll have to raise the alarm in a little while. If I don't, it's not just a scarred paw they'll give me. Do you see?"

Cold and heavy with sadness, Wolf licked his chops. He nodded slowly. "Yes," he said. "I do see. But I'll miss you, Calamity. So much."

"I'll miss you too, more than I can say." Rising, she pressed her elegant head to his neck. "But go, and go quickly. Please."

Wolf stayed for another moment, breathing in Calamity's warm scent one more time. Then he turned and bounded for the barn door and out into the yard. He couldn't bear to look back, so he kept running despite the pain in his injured paw, racing for the fence, seeking out the hole where he'd wriggled into the meadow what felt like a lifetime ago.

With my brother and my Pack. But they're not that anymore. I'll be on my own. But at least I'll be free. He dived for the hole.

No!

It had been stuffed full of fresh earth and stones; the soil was slightly loose but the grass was already growing over it. He knew he could never dig through it in time.

Another worry prickled at his fur.

Calamity needs to raise the alarm, and soon. I can't let more harm come to her—

Wolf twisted his head from side to side, searching desperately for an exit. *The sheep field!*

There was a rickety wooden shelter in one corner of it, next to a gnarled tree: a rough structure to protect the sheep from bad weather if they needed it. Wolf bounded for the meadow, skidded through the gate and dashed for the shelter.

It was perhaps the height of two sheep. Wolf did not hesitate, but raced faster as he approached its star-silvered outline. With one massive thrust of his haunches, he leaped, scrabbling onto its slanted roof.

Now he could hear furious barks, echoing through the yard, and the pounding of strong paws on flattened earth. They were coming for him, racing across the yard: four sets of paws. *Calamity raised the alarm. She'll be fine!*

But will I?

Wolf faced the fence. It wasn't high from the top of the sheep shelter, but there was wire with spines running along the top, and the tree branches were obstructing him.

Sundance's raging barks rang in his ears, much closer now, filled with hate. *He can't get me!*

Wolf leaped. His claws found an overhanging branch, and he hauled himself with raking claws onto it. His bushy tail snagged in a spine on the wire, but he tugged himself forward. The scents of the forest filled his nostrils now, and that something was calling to him again. *The hills, and the rivers, and the forests, and freedom—*

Jump, Wolf!

He plunged down just as Sundance's jaws snapped on his tail. Twisting, Wolf dragged himself free, and tumbled hard to the earth below, the forest litter breaking the worst of his fall. His coat was full of grit and soil and pine needles, but suddenly he didn't want to shake it off. The scent of sagebrush filled his head, and he could barely even hear Sundance's enraged squealing snarls.

Getting to his paws, Wolf glanced back through the fence

at the furious, howling Fierce Dogs. Their eyes were savage and murderous—all but one. Calamity was barking with the others but her eyes were soft and sad and happy all at once. He thought he could almost hear her voice inside his skull.

Good-bye, Wolf. Be happy.

He turned tail, and raced for the woods and for freedom.

CHAPTER TEN

The valley where he stood sloped down to a winding blue river fringed with trees and scrub. Farther away the forest grew denser, with pines and firs, until it blurred into hazy lilac mountains. Maybe his Pack was out there somewhere.

Maybe they are, but I won't be looking for them.

They'd abandoned him to the Fierce Dogs, thought Wolf. They'd betrayed him, and there was no going back.

I'm on my own.

Better that, he thought as he trotted down through the brush toward the valley floor, than to be back with the Rancher. He was lonely, but he knew it would pass. A shudder of sadness went through his gut when he thought of Calamity, but he would try not to think of her too often.

He missed Graceful, too. As he journeyed on through river

and forest, he found he even missed the Fierce Dogs; but he could shake that off quite easily. *It's just that they were a Pack,* he thought. *Not for long, but they were my Pack.*

He hoped he'd find another. He was no undisciplined Lone Wolf, snatching prey where he could find it.

The hunger in his stomach was more insistent than the vague sadness in his heart. In a patch of thorn scrub he sniffed out a rabbit, but when he sprang for it, it dodged and fled, zigzagging cunningly till he was forced to abandon the chase.

If I'd had a Pack, there would have been another wolf to flank it, block it, drive it back to me.

I'll manage.

The sun was lowering in the sky and his paw pads were beginning to ache when he heard something, somewhere off to his left: a high, squeaking bark of fear. Wolf came to a halt, hackles rising, ears pricking toward it.

It had been a long time since he'd heard the sound, but he knew a pup bark when he heard it. This one was afraid, very afraid. His brow furrowed. *Another wolf Pack? Where are they?*

For a moment he hesitated. He couldn't dash into the midst of a strange Pack; they'd simply kill him. But if there were other wolves near him, he had to try, at least, to join with them. Nerves fluttered in his belly, his need warring with wariness.

His ears flickered again, and he gave a low, uncertain growl. The pup was still yelping frantically. *Where's its Mother-Wolf? What is she waiting for?*

The pitch of the barking rose, almost to a squeal, and Wolf couldn't repress his instinct any longer. Blood raced to his heart and his belly and he shot forward, sprinting toward the sound of a pup in distress.

Branches slapped his muzzle and thorns snagged in his fur, but he ran on, the sound growing closer and louder. He could barely see where he was going, but now he could scent the pup ahead, its terror sharp in his nostrils. Still there were no sounds or smells of grown wolves, though there was something else. . . .

Plunging through a last belt of thorn-scrub, Wolf skidded to a halt.

And found himself nose-to-nose with an enormous, glossy giantfur.

Its rumbling roar made the ground shake. Wolf backed off swiftly, flattening his ears, as he took in what was happening.

The huge black giantfur shifted on its massive paws, giving him another roar of warning before turning back to its prey.

Beneath it, trapped between the roots of an ancient pine, cowered a terrified dog pup.

Rage drove out Wolf's fear. He lunged forward between the giantfur and the pup, backing against the tree. His legs jammed protectively over the pup, and he wrinkled his muzzle in a furious snarl.

The giantfur blinked and gave its hoarse roar again, making the tree shudder. Between Wolf's paws, the pup cringed, whimpering.

The giantfur went back on its hindpaws, baring sharp teeth in its small, pointed muzzle. Wolf's hackles bristled as he snarled back. Lunging forward, he snapped his fangs into its glossy black shoulder, deep enough to find flesh as well as fur.

The giantfur squealed in rage, then swiped enormous pale claws at Wolf. He fell back, but attacked again straightaway, nipping hard at the creature's neck. Once more he dodged back, slipping out of reach of those lashing claws.

Seeming uncertain now, the giantfur growled, its beady black eyes fixed on Wolf's. A low rumble came from its throat; then it snapped its teeth again. Wolf held his ground, fangs bared to the gums.

The giantfur's retreat was sudden and complete. It dropped

back to all fours, then turned and shambled into the bushes. Soon its growls faded and all Wolf could hear were the crash and snap of branches.

Wolf heaved a shuddering sigh of relief. Now that it was over, he could admit to himself how rash he'd been. A giantfur was no creature for a wolf to fight, let alone a dog.

He dipped his head quizzically to the pup shivering between his forelegs. "What did you do to annoy it?"

The pup was still shivering, but his huge eyes were bright with amazement and adoration. "That was the *best thing* I have *ever seen.*"

Wolf growled. "That was the stupidest thing you have ever seen. The giantfur could have killed us both. Where's your Pack?"

At once the pup's face fell. Or maybe it didn't, thought Wolf; maybe the pup's features were constantly sliding down its face. He was an odd-looking little thing, Wolf decided. His paws seemed clumsy and far too big for him, and his face was crumpled, his jaws floppy. Though his sturdy body was golden-brown, his face was black, and there were folds of wrinkled skin above his little black eyes. Maybe that was all that gave him his heavy-eyed, mournful expression.

The pup whimpered miserably. "I haven't got a Pack," he told him.

"What do you mean, you haven't got a Pack?" Wolf lifted his ears in surprise. "Every dog or wolf has a Pack." *Except me,* he reminded himself with a twinge of sadness. "What about your Mother-Dog?"

"My Mother-Dog got sick and died." Miserably the pup lowered his crinkled face to its forepaws. "So did my Sire-Dog. I'm all alone."

Wolf stared at him. A pup this size, left all alone in the forest? With giantfurs and coyotes and mountain sharpclaws? He was doomed.

"What's your name?" Wolf asked him.

"Snail." The pup raised his mournful-pup eyes to his.

Wolf choked on a laugh, and forced his face to look solemn. "I've heard some strange names lately, but *Snail?*"

"I like snails," said the pup dolefully. "They're tasty. And there's not much else around here."

Wolf sat back on his haunches, perplexed. "What are you going to do?"

The pup tilted his ugly crumpled head, fixing his eyes hopefully on Wolf. "I could come with you."

"I don't think so." Wolf shook his head. "I don't have a Pack either. I wouldn't be able to look after you—I've got enough trouble looking after myself at the moment."

The pup wriggled, and crept tighter beneath his belly, so that Wolf had to crane to look down at him.

"But I could look after you," he whined, nuzzling into Wolf. "I'm quite fast for a pup, even my Sire-Dog said so. We could be a Pack together! I could be your lookout. I could find the prey, and chase it to you, and you can kill it!"

Wolf peered at the little thing, dumbfounded. "I don't know...."

The pup poked his head out from beneath him, his eyes pleading. "I could find you *lots* of snails."

Wolf whuffed with laughter, he couldn't help it. Then he grew thoughtful again. *He's a pup and he's helpless. You can't leave him out here. And snails aren't that bad....*

"I suppose you could come with me for a little while," he told the pup doubtfully. "Just for a bit, though. And you have to do everything I tell you. No fooling around or disobeying me. And no pestering giantfurs."

"Yay!" The pup bounced out from beneath his legs, wagging his hindquarters furiously. "I promise, I promise! I'll be *so good!*"

Oh, Great Wolf, what have I let myself in for? But Wolf couldn't help a tingle of amusement. "You'd better be."

"I will!" The pup sat down suddenly, panting. "What's your name?"

My Name, thought Wolf. *My Name?*

He could say *Wolf,* the last name he'd been given. Or should he say *Dog?* It was the Name his Pack had given him under the full moon, in sight of the Great Wolf; the Name his Mother-Wolf had told him to be proud of.

A breeze stirred the foliage as the pup gazed expectantly up at him. On it, he could smell the mountains, the firs, and the sage-brush.

I don't have to be either of those things, he realized. *Both my Packs are gone. Maybe it's time to choose my own identity. Live as myself, and for myself. Find my own friends and family and respect. Protect the wolves and dogs that I want to protect.*

Maybe I can make a Pack of my own.

He felt his spine stiffen with determination. Gazing into Snail's eager eyes, he drew himself up proudly and gave the pup a wolf grin.

"You can call me Alpha."

SWEET'S JOURNEY

PACK LIST

SWIFT-DOG PACK

<u>ALPHA:</u>

    large male swift-dog with brown-and-white fur

<u>BETA:</u>

    sandy-colored female swift-dog (also known as Callie)

    SWEET—small female swift-dog with short gray fur

    BROOK—black male swift-dog with very long legs

    ROCKET—young gray-and-white male swift-dog

    FLEET—elderly brown female swift-dog with white paws

<u>OMEGA:</u>

    small black-and-white female swift-dog

CHAPTER ONE

Not my eyes, Callie! Not my eyes . . .

Sweet ducked and twisted out of reach just as the Beta lashed out her claws, the tip of one catching Sweet's cheekbone. Knocked off-balance, Sweet fell and rolled, then sprang back to her paws, snarling defiance, her fur and hackles prickling. She could feel blood beading on her face. *If Callie's claw had found my eyeball . . . She* shuddered.

Sweet gave her pelt a firm shake as the two of them circled each other warily, but she couldn't lose the tingling rage and frustration. In a challenge like this one—a challenge between dogs of the same Pack—aiming for a dog's eyes was forbidden. It wasn't just a vicious move, it was a stupid one. No dog wanted a Pack member maimed! And for swift-dogs like them, eyesight mattered even more. They were so fleet, so quick on their paws, they all needed their keen vision intact in a chase.

That didn't seem to matter to Callie. *The Beta wanted to win at all costs,* Sweet realized.

But there was another Pack rule Sweet didn't intend to break: no dog whined and cowered and complained about their opponent's tactics in a challenge. The whole Pack was watching this fight.

Sweet curled the skin back from her muzzle, revealing her teeth. Callie was not going to get the better of her, and that meant the Beta wasn't going to send Sweet whining to their Alpha, either. . . .

Callie bunched her muscles and sprang again. Sweet lunged to meet her in midair.

Although it went against all her instincts, she closed her eyes, letting her other senses guide her. She could feel Callie's body right there, and the stir of her hot breath as the Beta snapped and bit at Sweet's face. Sweet spun and twisted, then sank her teeth into fur and flesh.

Yes! Opening her eyes, she realized her jaws were clamped on the side of Callie's neck. Taking advantage of the other dog's flinch, she flung her whole slender weight against Callie, and the Beta slipped and fell with Sweet on top, pinned to the ground.

I won, Sweet thought, panting through her mouthful of fur as she straddled Callie's flank. I finally beat her!

But Callie wasn't finished yet. She writhed and heaved, sending Sweet tumbling aside, and in moments Sweet was sprawled on the damp earth, the breath knocked out of her lungs. This time Callie was the dog on top, and her jaws were clamped on Sweet's scruff, holding her down. There was a light of hate in the

Beta's eyes, and a chill swept through Sweet's blood along with the fury. Curse Callie!

But the awful chill that immobilized her didn't drain away. It filled Sweet's body, and seemed to seep out into the air around the two fighting dogs. It was instinct, warning her. . . .

Sweet shuddered. She remembered what happened next. And the fight wasn't the worst thing that had happened that day . . . the day of the Big Growl. . . .

The longpaws came from nowhere, and everywhere. They were all around the Pack, as if they'd been hiding inside the very trees. Instantly Callie released Sweet, and they both lined up with their Packmates, growling their defiance at the longpaws.

Every muscle and bone in her body urged Sweet to run. Turn! Run! Go! They were swift-dogs, weren't they? The longpaws were slow and clumsy. The dogs could all flee, right now, and if the rest wouldn't—Sweet could! She could run far away, faster than any longpaw—

But the Pack was snarling and eyeing the longpaws that closed in from all sides. The Pack wanted to fight, to meet the longpaws' challenge and defeat them.

Madness! But if Sweet bolted—if she made a run for it—surely the others would follow. . . .

She couldn't battle the urge any longer. Spinning, Sweet fled, her speed carrying her away from the sticks and nets and the long flailing paws of the *creatures looking to capture the dogs.*

A moment later, Sweet skidded to a brief halt to look back. Her Pack . . . they weren't following! They stood their ground against the longpaws, and panic flooded through Sweet's belly. Raising her voice, she howled to them in dismay and grief.

Follow me! Follow me! Run with me *now*—

Her own broken howl jolted her out of sleep. Dazed, Sweet shook away the fuzziness of waking and hauled herself onto her fore-paws. Her heart thrashed in her narrow chest and her fur was on end all over her body, but there were no longpaws here. No long-paws, no swift-dogs, no *Pack.* It had been a dream, that was all.

No, not a dream: a memory. A terrible memory.

Why? she thought miserably. *Why do I always have to dream about the day I ran?*

Slowly Sweet got to her paws, sniffing the strange air. The grass and earth were soft beneath her paw pads, and there was no metal wire caging her in, no walls to stop her from running. This meadow was so much better than the Trap House, yet it wasn't a truly wild place. All around her, Sweet could feel the work of longpaws. The trees stood in ordered ranks, like dogs lined up for a battle. The grass was clipped and smooth, and the glinting river was channeled under a stone bridge that had been built with long, hairless paws. The air itself made Sweet's fur prickle.

It was a good enough place to sleep for one night, but it was no place for a wild swift-dog to live—especially a dog with no Pack. Remembering that she was alone now sent a shiver through Sweet's bones. She'd move on at once, she thought, a whine of sadness rising in her throat.

She missed Lucky already. How could he have let her go? How could he *want* to be alone, in this new world of all worlds? The kind, smart, golden-furred dog she'd met in the Trap House had insisted all along that he was a Lone Dog, but she hadn't quite believed him—not till he'd refused to come with her on her journey away from the destroyed city.

Sweet clenched her fangs in angry bewilderment. Lucky's attitude was madness; it was something she'd never understand, not till the day she went to the Earth-Dog. How could a dog not *want* to find a Pack? And Sweet knew she would find one: if not today, then tomorrow, or the next day. How could Lucky refuse to come with her to the forest? Ridiculous! There would be dogs there. There would be a Pack she could join to find new strength, a Pack she could help by adding her own strength to theirs. That was the way of dogs; it was what dogs were *for*!

A little tremor of fear went through her belly. Maybe she shouldn't even have paused to rest in this strange longpaw meadow. Perhaps any dogs who had left the city would have trekked too far by now; perhaps she would never catch up with them. The very thought made Sweet shiver.

No, she reassured herself. A Pack needed a camp, and once dogs found a safe place to make their territory, they'd stay there. As long as her nose didn't let her down, she'd find them; she was sure of it.

Sweet couldn't resist breaking into a steady, swift lope as she headed for the forest. Already she could smell it: the rich scent of pine needles and rotting leaves and damp, cool hollows. No clear dog-scents yet, but she was confident those would come. She had only to reach those dense trees that stretched for countless chases, and she'd find a Pack.

She *had* to find a Pack.

At the edge of the forest she didn't even hesitate, but leaped over a fallen log and ran into its darkness, darting and dodging through the thick ranks of pine and aspen. Her heart beat harder and faster as she plunged deeper into the trees, and not just because of her swift-dog pace. There *were* dog-scents here, and lots of them.

Hopelessly confused and jumbled dog-scents.

Each time Sweet lowered her slender nose to catch a whiff of a dog and follow its trail, she would lose it, distracted and misled by other trails that overlaid it. She would follow the stronger scent, only to lose it again among other scent-markers. Many dogs had passed through the forest—perhaps too many, she realized with a quiver of panic. How would she ever find and follow a clear trail in this maze of smells?

The whole world was tangled and turned upside down, that was the problem. But as soon as she thought that, Sweet felt oddly reassured. The Big Growl had turned the world into a place of madness and confusion, and of course things would not be as easy as they'd once been. What mattered, she told herself confidently, was that there were *dogs*. At any moment she'd find a strong trail and follow it, and she'd find a new Pack that needed her contribution. And as soon as she had a Pack, the craziness of the world wouldn't matter. Pack was everything.

There were other scents to distract her, Sweet realized as she paused to sniff at a pine's exposed roots. Smaller, darker, sharper trails, made by scurrying prey. Her empty belly rumbled, and hunger nipped at her.

I'll think better with a full belly.

Making her decision, she reluctantly abandoned the dog-scents for the moment and began to nose her way along one of the stronger prey-trails. Slowing, placing her paws with care, she scanned the undergrowth, her ears pricked forward. *Be silent, Sweet. You're hunting alone . . . for now. . . .*

There! A movement in the undergrowth. A vole; Sweet caught a glimpse of its russet back and its short tail. It saw her, and darted for the shelter of the forest litter, but Sweet was fast, and she was hungry. She shot forward and snatched it up in her jaws, crunching and gulping it down, bones, tail and all.

It was small, she thought as she licked her jaws, but big enough to take the edge off her hunger.

A new sense of urgency drove her on now, her trotting stride rapid, and she hadn't gone many rabbit-chases before she broke once more into a loping run. Her nose searched every hint of breeze, every stir of the dank forest air, and her heart clenched tight. *What if I never find those dogs?*

The scent hit her quite suddenly, filling her nostrils, and she came to a halt, head raised.

It was a scent she recognized from earlier in the day, but it seemed clearer and stronger now; perhaps it was just that she had had the sense to fill her belly. Sweet focused hard on the messages it brought her, and she drew in a sudden, hopeful breath.

That's a swift-dog! I'm sure of it!

In an instant, visions of her life with the swift-dog Pack flitted across the eye of her mind, sending pangs of regret through her. Callie the Beta had bullied and intimidated her, it was true, but Sweet had been loyal to her Pack; she had loved them. The memory of her Packmates being rounded up for the Trap House, the echoes of their howls as they were captured, filled her head with chaos and misery, and Sweet had to crouch down in the dry fallen leaves, pressing herself close against the ground and flattening her ears.

She and Lucky had been the only dogs to make it out of that Trap House alive when the Big Growl struck. She had been certain of it. . . .

But now, she wasn't so sure.

Is every one of my Packmates truly dead? Sweet realized she didn't know, and she didn't even want to believe it. *Maybe some of them escaped the longpaws. Maybe some of them were never captured at all. . . .*

There was no choice to be made; she had to follow this scent. Sweet sprang to her feet, and set off at a run again. If any of her Packmates were still alive, she *had* to track them down. The recognition was followed instantly by a horrible bolt of shame.

I ran.

Of course I ran. I'm a swift-dog, it's what I was born for. . . .

But I ran when my Pack was in trouble, and the longpaws caught me on my own.

If she hadn't fled like a coward, Sweet realized, she'd know what had happened; she'd know whether any of her Pack had escaped the longpaws' attack. She'd have shared their fate. Maybe they'd have all died, been crushed in the collapse of the Trap House, but at least they'd have been *together*.

My Pack.

Desperately she raced on, following the scent almost blindly, so when the trees ended suddenly in a bright expanse of meadow, she skidded, shocked. The sun was bright overhead, dazzling her eyes after the shadows of the forest, and she could hear the sound of running water.

Flanks heaving, Sweet sniffed the air. *The river!* She was so thirsty . . . and she remembered how her Pack had loved to swim. They'd splashed and swum in the cool, clear stream sent by the River-Dog, the stream that washed grit and grime from a dog's fur and soothed aching paw pads. . . .

Sweet trotted eagerly toward the bank, but within a rabbit-chase of the water's edge she halted. The delicate scent of the river was overlaid with something stronger, something unpleasant. As she drew closer it stung her nostrils, making her wrinkle her muzzle and back away.

Her stomach churned as she stared at the rippling stream, flecked now with yellow foam. Was the river sick?

Uncertainly she began to pace along the bank, angling her head away from the water to avoid the increasing stench. Even the dry tightness in her throat couldn't persuade her to lap at that sickly scum. *But if I want to go farther, I'll need to cross the water. Is it safe to swim in it?*

With a rush of relief, she saw ahead of her one of the longpaw bridges that crossed stretches of water. It didn't look as new and solid as the one she'd seen that morning. The timber was damp in places, dark with rot, and the whole thing swayed alarmingly as the torrent beat against it—but it was at least in one piece.

Sweet glanced back at her flanks. She'd never been a heavy or even a sturdy sort of dog, and now her ribs showed clearly through her hide. Even so, she wasn't sure the fragile bridge would hold her weight.

But what choice do I have? Sweet sighed inwardly.

I need a Pack so badly. I have to try. . . .

After all, hadn't that swift-dog—the one whose scent she'd

caught—made it over the bridge? She could smell its scent, leading her across. If she wanted to reach that dog, Sweet had to follow. Catching her breath, she placed a tentative paw on the first shaky planks.

It seemed to sag under her slender weight, but as she set another paw beside the first, the bridge settled and steadied. One by one, she brought her hindpaws onto the surface too, and stood still for a moment, trembling.

Every muscle in her body tensed as she edged forward, ready to leap back at the first sign of collapse. One glance at the rushing water below her, scum-flecked and oddly yellowish, made Sweet more certain than ever that she didn't want to fall in.

Beneath her creeping paws, the bridge groaned, and she stopped, one paw in the air. *Don't startle it,* she told herself.

One more step, and she heard a terrible screeching creak behind her. Hardly daring to look back, she stopped again, heart slamming against her ribs. *It's going to fall. . . .*

Slowly she craned her head around, pricking her ears with anxiety, and she felt a sinking sensation like a stone in her belly.

I've come too far across! I can't *go back.*

There was only one thing for it: *go forward*. Panting, Sweet bunched her muscles, her whole body quivering. Briefly she shut her eyes, then snapped them open.

Springing forward, Sweet bolted, running as she'd never run before. She could barely feel the rotting wood beneath her paws; she could only hear the creak and rumble and splash as chunks of the bridge fell away behind and beneath her. She was sure she was running on nothing but thin air, her claws scrabbling for purchase, her panting breath stabbing like teeth in her chest. As the roar of collapse filled her ears, she leaped for the bank.

Sweet crashed to the solid ground on her flank, legs still flailing, but she'd made it. And only just in time. Rolling over and stumbling to her paws, she saw the foaming water engulf the shattered bridge as the River-Dog gulped it greedily down.

Oh, River-Dog, you must have been hungry. . . .

Still panting for breath, her chest aching, Sweet dipped her head and closed her eyes. *Thank you, River-Dog, for letting me cross before you ate the bridge.*

As the shock faded, a whine of unhappiness built inside her, escaping at last in a choked whimper.

And River-Dog? If my friend Lucky comes to you? Please, please find a way to let him cross too. . . .

CHAPTER TWO

The Sun-Dog was slinking alarmingly close to the horizon behind her as Sweet padded on, her paws aching with every step. The sky ahead had darkened to a grayish blue, but there was still enough light for her to make out the terrible wounds in the earth.

She skirted them widely whenever she caught sight of one, her fur bristling, her heart pounding. The scars were scratched deep in the ground, and some plunged so far down into blackness, Sweet couldn't make out where they ended. They were jagged and horrible, as if some monster had dug its claws into the land and torn out its insides.

And a monster *had* done just that, Sweet realized in horror. The Big Growl had inflicted these dreadful wounds.

Poor Earth-Dog. She must be in such pain. . . .

Sweet's nostrils twitched. Ahead of her there was the smell of old and dead fires, like the cold remnants of a forest blaze, but fainter. She could only press on, but she moved with much more caution now, her eyes peering ahead into the dimming twilight. Old cinders and ashes were not the only scent that reached her. There was a frightening tang, strong but fading, of longpaws.

Every sense alert, every muscle tensed to run, Sweet crept closer to the source of the odors. *I have to go through this place. There's no other way to find that swift-dog.*

She jerked back, hackles rising, as she nearly trod in a shallow pit. Wrinkling her muzzle, she sniffed at it. Blackened ash and charred logs, but they were cold and dead. Glancing around, she noticed more small pits, and planks of wood raised up on legs. *The kind of place a longpaw would sit.* But why would longpaws make small fires in the forest?

There was no sign or sound of longpaws, though; only their fading smell, so Sweet forced herself to pad on through the darkening evening. Beyond a line of trees she saw the faint glint of light on metal, and she paused to sniff the air.

They were loudcages, she realized—huge ones, their black rubber paws motionless and overgrown with grass. There was no smell of the fire-juice that the longpaws fed their smaller loudcages. Feeling a little more confident, Sweet crept forward and eased between two of the huge cages.

There was no movement at all. In the flank of the one on her left, a flap of metal swung open, creaking in the light breeze.

Gathering her courage, Sweet climbed carefully up the metal steps that led to the hole, and poked her head cautiously inside the loudcage. Still there was no sign of life. The loudcage smelled strongly of longpaws; their furs had been left draped across seats and hanging on hooks, and there was a trace of a food-smell. Not an especially nice food-smell, thought Sweet as she nosed at a gaping door; it reminded her of spoil-boxes in the city, with their reek of rot and decay. The longpaws must have made a den inside this cold and empty cage.

What strange creatures the longpaws were. . . .

She shivered. There was nothing for her here. She'd rather hunt for herself, alone, than trust the longpaws' abandoned food. Backing out of the loudcage and down the metal steps, she shook herself and trotted quickly on between two rows of the huge loudcages. As she passed one beast, the familiar swift-dog scent struck her nostrils, making her paws falter.

It was so much stronger now. Stronger, and terribly familiar . . .

Callie!

Changing direction, Swift trotted on into the trees beyond

the loudcages. She had to find her former Beta, though she hoped very much that there were other swift-dogs with Callie. Would her old enemy even be happy to see Sweet? She doubted it.

Her paw steps slowed, uncertain, as the scent grew stronger. No, there were no other dogs here—and Callie's trail was still. The Beta had not moved for a while. Sweet cocked her head, curious and alert.

Was that a whimper?

If Callie's hurt, she won't be able to help me. And I might not be able to do anything for her. I could just walk away. . . .

No, she realized, with a jolt. *That's not the kind of dog I am. I'm a Pack Dog, and Packmates don't abandon each other. No matter what.*

The decision gave her new courage. Pacing forward into the tree shadows, she saw a shape lying quite still, its flanks moving jerkily with each shallow breath.

"Callie?" Sweet murmured hesitantly.

The dog raised its head, ears coming forward, but the eyes were bright with pain and resentment.

"Callie, it *is* you."

Callie whimpered, wincing with pain at even the small movement. Then her voice lowered to a disdainful growl, and her muzzle curled.

117

"Well, if it isn't Sweet. The dog who ran away," she sneered. "Want a fight, do you? I'm sure you'll be able to beat me now. Coward."

Sweet took a breath. Callie's words were like a claw in her gut, and she almost wished the Beta was fit enough to attack her physically. That might have hurt less. And the sting of Callie's accusation was all the worse for being true. In the Pack's moment of greatest peril, Sweet had turned tail and fled.

She swallowed hard. "I'm not here to fight you, Callie."

"Oh? In that case, you might as well go ahead and mock me. I won't be fighting again." Callie's muzzle peeled back from her fangs.

"I wouldn't do that either." Sweet padded forward and around to Callie's side. Still the wounded swift-dog didn't move, and Sweet took a breath when she saw the deep gash in Callie's flank. Worse, one of her hind legs flopped uselessly to the side, crushed and bleeding. Sweet blinked, overwhelmed by pity.

"Don't look at me like that," snarled Callie.

Composing herself, Sweet tried to sound matter-of-fact. "What happened, Callie?"

"You get to call me Callie now, do you?" the swift-dog sneered. "Because I'm not your Beta anymore? You would not dare be so insolent if I could *move*."

"The reason you're not my Beta is because our Pack is gone,"
snapped Sweet, then calmed herself again. There was nothing to
be gained from a squabble. She tried again: "What happened?"

Callie grunted. "I escaped from the Trap House. Like you, I
suppose. I thought you'd died with the rest. I came through the
forest, crossed the river; I did *all that*. And then I made the mistake
of smelling food in one of these cursed things." She jerked her
head at the nearest loudcage. "Tried to climb into its belly. It lost
its balance and fell on top of me. So much for my swift-dog speed,
eh? I'll never run again."

"Callie." Sweet dipped her nose to lick her old Beta's ear. "I'm
so sorry."

For a moment Callie was silent, then at last she said gruffly: "I
won't even walk again. I'm done for, Sweet."

Sweet nuzzled her, unable to think of anything to say.

"I was once a racing dog, you know," said Callie dreamily, after
a long silence. "I would run for longpaws. They liked that. They
liked to see us swift-dogs run in a circle, chasing a dead hare. As
if we thought it lived, and we could catch it. Ha! We liked to win,
that was all. Never mind the longpaws; we hated them anyway. It
was each other we raced for. We were slaves to the longpaws, but

among our Pack we had honor."

"I'm sure you did," murmured Sweet.

"They gave us our names. 'Callie' is short for some ridiculous longpaw word, you know? *California Dreamer,* they called me. Ridiculous name; who needs one so long? I was 'Callie' to my Pack." Her eyes grew misty. "It's been a good name."

"A very fine name." *For a fine dog,* Sweet wanted to add, but she didn't think Callie would appreciate it. Her old Beta might think she was mocking her. Sweet felt a surge of unexpected grief.

"When we stopped being any use to the longpaws, they'd abandon us," Callie went on. "That was when I started to be happy." She gave a gruff laugh. "But they had other animals, animals that did the same as us. Ran in circles. Because the longpaws liked it. And the longpaws would do worse than abandon them."

"What animals?" Sweet pricked her ears forward, curious.

"Horses. You heard of those? No, didn't think you would. They're bigger than us, but just as breakable." Callie gave her crushed leg a filthy glare. "Big bodies on skinny legs, those horses. They'd break a leg, sometimes. Then the longpaws would get out their loudsticks and shoot them in the head."

"*Shoot* them?" Sweet blinked, mystified.

"I don't know exactly what it means, but that was the word.

The loudsticks spat something that killed them. No use, a horse that can't run. I used to think it was cruel," Callie mused thoughtfully. "But you know what, Sweet?"

"What?"

"I wouldn't mind a longpaw with a loudstick right now."

"Callie, don't say that!" Sweet licked her face desperately.

"What else would I say? Listen to me." Callie twisted her head to glare into Sweet's eyes. "I'll never run again. I'm never going to *walk*. You've had my neck in your jaws before, Sweet. Finish what you started then. Sink your teeth into my throat and get this *over with*."

Sweet shivered and backed away, whining softly. "I can't do that, Callie. I could never do that."

"Why not? You hate me, don't you?"

"I hate no dog!" barked Sweet fiercely, still backing away.

"There you go again." Callie's lip curled back from her teeth. "Running away from your problems."

Sweet hesitated, then crept back to Callie's side. She lay down, careful not to brush the terrible wound in the Beta's flank. "Callie, I won't kill you. But I'm not running away. Am I?"

Callie sighed, lowering her muzzle to her forepaws. "No. No, I don't suppose you are. You're a good dog, Sweet. Don't laugh.

I've always known you were a good dog. A better dog than me."

"Don't say—" But Sweet stopped as Callie gave an agonized whimper of pain. "Callie?"

Callie sucked in a breath, and her sides heaved. The movement opened up the wound even more, and Sweet felt a gush of new, warm blood against her flank. Shocked, she licked Callie's wound, very gently. Then she shifted away, afraid of hurting her.

"Would you mind moving 'round to the other side?" Callie's growl was barely audible. "You can lie against me there. I'm cold."

Sweet slunk around to Callie's other flank, so that she could no longer see the blood pooling beside her old Beta's body. She lay down again, pressing close to Callie, and heard the swift-dog give a soft growl of gratitude.

"Callie?" Sweet murmured quietly, pressing her nose gently to the other dog's shoulder.

There was no sound, though Callie's flanks stirred for a while, in and out with shallow breaths. Callie didn't speak again, and Sweet barely noticed the moment when the gentle movement of her rib cage stopped altogether.

CHAPTER THREE

I never really cared for Callie, thought Sweet, gazing back numbly at the swift-dog's motionless body. *But I never wanted this to happen.*

She sat back on her haunches, gathering her thoughts, not wanting to abandon her former Beta quite yet. *It's the Big Growl,* she realized with a chill of dread. *Everything has changed because of it. We don't know who our friends and our enemies are. We don't even know if the Spirit Dogs are on our side.*

It had been bad enough imagining her Pack dying in the carnage and chaos of the Trap House; actually watching Callie die had twisted Sweet's insides with horror. And now she felt more alone than ever. *Is this what happened to them all? Every single one of my Packmates—have they all gone to the Earth-Dog the way Callie just did?*

Oh, I miss Lucky even more. . . .

But there was no way of getting back to him, she realized. She'd probably lost the City Dog's scent, and his company, forever.

What was more, the bridge was gone, and the River-Dog wouldn't let her cross back—if the River-Dog even cared anymore what happened to her. River-Dog was probably concerned only with her own terrible sickness.

We're all on our own from now on. But if the Spirit Dogs can't or won't help us, that makes it all the more vital to find a Pack.

With one last sad look at Callie's remains, Sweet turned and plodded away, following the same stars as before. There was no point going back; she could only press on. The stars seemed so much farther away now, though, and the night felt colder.

Sweet did her best not to run, knowing she should save her energy. Short, sharp bursts of speed would do her no good here; how far she would have to travel, no dog knew. But still her muscles and paw pads ached by the time the Sun-Dog rose behind her.

By his low, golden light she could clearly see more of those cruel gashes in the earth as she traveled on. They were worse even than the wound in Callie's flank, the wound she'd died of. Was Earth-Dog dying too, Sweet wondered?

How can she possibly survive this?

A black misery settled over her, but it lifted just a little when she crested the rise of a grassy knoll and saw a line of distant lilac hills. If she could reach that high ground, she might be able to spot her old Pack's territory.

Though I doubt I'll find any of my old friends. Sweet heaved a sigh of grief, then shook herself. *Callie and I survived the Trap House. Maybe some of the others did . . . ? Even one . . . ?*

As she forced her aching legs to move, every step jolting her slender joints, she began to catch dog-scents again, and her ears pricked with hope. At the same time, her skin tingled, alert to the chance of danger. The scents grew thicker and more numerous the farther she walked, and there were none she recognized. Every tree and every rock was thick with dog-markers, filling her nostrils with overpowering messages, and Sweet knew this must be the territory of a Pack.

I will have to be submissive to get through this territory in search of my friends. Nerves jangled beneath her fur. *Be careful, Sweet, be wise . . . and be humble.*

Taking a deep breath, she paused, then headed for the dark line that marked the beginning of a forest. She didn't want to be caught unawares. Sweet placed each delicate paw with care, her ears alert for the slightest noise, the tiniest movement in the shadows.

Her caution was unnecessary. With a crashing of undergrowth, a muscular red dog bounded out of the trees and stood foursquare, growling and glaring at Sweet.

"Stop right there, intruder. No dog trespasses on our land!"

Sweet swallowed hard, lowering her forequarters and wagging her tail. "I'm sorry. I don't mean to trespass."

The red dog's lip curled. "Then what are you doing here?"

Sweet let her tongue loll, trying to look as friendly as she could. "I'm looking for my own Pack, that's all. Have you seen any other dogs like me?"

The red dog gave a bark of laughter. Her eyes were narrow and contemptuous. "Like you? There are no dogs like you on this territory. They wouldn't survive!" She paced forward, circling Sweet and sniffing at her disdainfully. "You're skinny. You're weak. Any dogs like you will have taken a very wide path around, because our Pack doesn't tolerate weaklings. Are you prepared to fight your way through us?"

Sweet turned her head to watch the red dog. She was frightened, but she didn't want to make any sudden moves. "All I want is to pass through here. I'll keep moving, I promise. And I wouldn't dream of hunting on your territory."

The red dog laughed again. "As if we'd let you!"

It seemed so horribly unfair and unreasonable, after all she'd been through. Sweet clenched her jaws to stop herself growling.

As the red dog walked around to face her directly once more, Sweet slowly stood upright, meeting her gaze defiantly.

An expression of surprise crossed the red dog's face, but then her muzzle curled. She ground her forepaws into the earth, her shoulder muscles bunching for an attack—but at that moment, a pale shape appeared in the trees behind her.

Sweet took a single step back, startled but curious. Her nose twitched at the new dog's strange scent. As he came forward, the red dog's attitude seemed to change instantly. Her head dipped slightly in submission, her hackles lowered and the aggression melted away as she stepped aside.

He must *be her Alpha,* thought Sweet. *He has all the power here—it's as clear as the scent-markings on the boundary trees.*

He was a massive creature, as close to a wolf as Sweet had ever seen. His shaggy fur was rippling shades of black, gray, and white, and his eyes glowed yellow and fierce, but without the snarling aggression of the red dog. Behind him came an even bigger dog, burly and blunt-faced, and a much smaller white-and-tan female with a mean expression.

"Who's this, Beta? And what is her business in my territory?" The half wolf's rumbling voice seemed to silence every sound in the forest.

Sweet ducked her head quickly and respectfully, opening her jaws to respond, but the red dog got there before her.

"She's begging for passage through the woods. Can't survive without her friends," she sneered. "Though I doubt they've survived anyway. We should get rid of her—drive her back where she came from. It will be kinder in the long run, Alpha."

Sweet gathered her dignity and stood straighter, ignoring the red dog to address the half wolf directly.

"I don't mean to cause trouble," she told him, quietly but firmly. "And I won't. If you're willing to let me pass through your territory, I won't hunt. You can send a dog with me as an escort, to make sure."

The half wolf said nothing for long moments; he just examined her with that piercing yellow gaze. Sweet couldn't suppress the tremor that went through her muscles, but she managed not to let it show. The whole forest seemed to hold its breath until at last the half wolf gave an upward jerk of his head.

"Very well." There was a look in his eyes she couldn't quite read. "Fiery here will escort you through to the far edge of our territory. But don't get your hopes up. There have been no other swift-dogs in the forest that I've seen—and I see everything."

"Which doesn't mean," snarled the red dog, in obvious annoyance at the Alpha's concession, "that you can come crawling back to us when you fail. We've enough mouths to feed without a useless creature like you."

Sweet expected the Alpha to confirm his Beta's sentiments, but to her surprise he said nothing. He swung his great head to stare at the red dog. After only moments, the Beta averted her eyes and licked her jaws, scowling.

"I won't be back," said Sweet proudly. "I won't be a burden to any Pack, believe me. I'm looking for dogs like me—a Pack that's *welcoming.*"

A hint of amusement crossed the Alpha's stern face, and his muzzle wrinkled. He knew full well, thought Sweet, that her remarks were aimed at his Beta. The red dog was silent, but her hackles bristled.

With a last nod to the Alpha, Sweet followed the burly dog Fiery as he led her into the forest, following clear dog-trails that hinted at a well-established, well-organized Pack. Fiery's sheer size was intimidating, but Sweet found that she wasn't scared of him. He murmured an occasional word to guide or reassure her, but on the whole was amiably silent for the whole long trek, till

Sweet saw a stretch of water glint between pine trunks.

Fiery led her to its edge, then jerked his head toward it.

"Here," he said gruffly. "We're nearly at the edge of our lands, and you'd better have a drink to keep you going. It'll be a long walk before you find any other dogs."

"Thanks," she told him, dipping her muzzle to drink. The water was cold and clear and pure, and it tasted of the earth and the forest. Sweet shivered as she remembered the sick river she'd had to cross, and she closed her eyes briefly to thank the River-Dog for bringing her to better water. She drank for a long time, reminded suddenly of how thirsty she was.

"I wish you good luck," growled Fiery, gazing across to the distant forest beyond the lake. "I hope you do find a few of your Pack. It's been a bad time for all dogs."

"Thank you," said Sweet. She licked her chops and padded carefully into the water, cooling her paws. "I have to hope some of them survived."

The big dog nodded slowly. "Our Pack lost a few dogs in the Big Growl too. I'm sorry we couldn't be more welcoming, but every dog is afraid. Who knows if the bad times are over?"

Sweet turned her head to watch his eyes, and when she saw the fear in them, her own anxiety sparked into new life. If a dog so powerful could still fear the Big Growl's return, what hope was there for a fragile swift-dog? She shivered.

"I hope the bad days *are* over," she told him softly. "But I don't think any dog can trust that they are."

CHAPTER FOUR

Sweet was stunned at the chaos she found beyond the half wolf's territory. She and her Pack had lived in what she'd thought was *the wild,* but here in the more remote forest it was as if all the order of the world had been destroyed, as if the Spirit Dogs had abandoned the land to ruin. Mighty trees had toppled like saplings, their branches broken and the leaves stripped and scattered. Great rips had been opened in the earth, ragged and yawning, and massive rocks had tumbled loose from their sockets, crushing plants and creatures alike. There were signs of scorching, as if Lightning had leaped to the earth over and over again in a panic, and some stretches of ground were charred wastelands.

Sweet's nostrils flared in dismay. There were so many small corpses crushed here, so much carrion, even the crows couldn't keep up. Fat and sleek—unlike the other forest creatures—they hopped and strutted and flapped onto fallen branches, cocking their black heads arrogantly to watch her pass.

Earth-Dog, were you really so angry with us all? You haven't even consumed the dead. . . .

Sweet was glad to leave the low-lying, destroyed land, to feel the ground begin to rise beneath her paws once more, and as the trees thinned she felt a new urgency and energy. She bounded up the last slope to the crest of a sparsely treed ridge, and gazed out across open country, letting the stiff breeze bring its many scents to her nostrils.

But there were no dog-scents she could trace. Sweet's ears lowered in disappointment. There was nothing but the smell of the forest, and the distant reek of the sick river, reaching even as far as this. There was certainly no sign of land she recognized from her Pack's former camp.

The longpaws must have taken us far from our home when they caught us, she realized miserably. *I've no idea where to go from here. I've no idea if there's a home left that's worth finding.*

A ball of rage swelled in her gut, and Sweet gave in to it. Lifting her narrow head, she gave a furious bark.

"Why, Sky-Dogs? Why did you do this to us? Earth-Dog, what did we do wrong?"

Of course there was no answer, only the moan of the wind in

the trees and the heedless song of birds.

"If I understood, I might feel better!" she howled.

Silence. Sweet sat back on her haunches, tucking her tail tightly beneath her, and stared out at the distant hills, and the amber glow of the drowsy Sun-Dog as he settled for the night.

If I wasn't alone, it wouldn't be so bad. Lucky, why did you have to be so stubborn?

She missed the City Dog more and more, with a deep keen ache. It was odd, when she'd known him for such a short time, but he'd been strong when she needed him. And clever, and funny, and kind.

And stupid! With all his Lone Dog nonsense!

She gave a sharp bark of irritation, then a soft unhappy whine; then at last she got to her paws and shook herself. Whatever she thought of Lucky's foolish notions, she had to follow his example. She was a Lone Dog for now, whether she wanted to be or not. So it was time to be strong, and look after herself.

The Moon-Dog was rising, clearer now that the Sun-Dog's light was dying, and the sky ahead was darkest blue. *I need to get going. I'll survive this, all of it.*

But where will I go?

The Moon-Dog's eye was full and round and white, huge against the twinkling stars. Sweet took a breath suddenly, cocking an ear, straining to listen.

Yes. Drifting on the light wind from far away, rising and falling, she could hear the echoing voices of a Pack singing to the Moon-Dog. *A Great Howl,* she thought, and longing tugged at her heart.

She remembered her own Pack's Howls, that sense of being *one* despite their petty daytime squabbles, the strong blood call of kinship and loyalty. She remembered how the real world seemed to fall away as they lifted their voices to the night, how she could sense the Wind-Dogs racing between them all, dodging and flying and howling with joy. She'd felt as if she herself was running, too, though she sat motionless among her friends, as if the Wind- Dogs were as one with all of them. Was that how other dogs felt? *I want to Howl again,* she thought. *I want to be one with a Pack.* . . .

The eerie distant howling thrilled into her blood, filling her with a new determination. She thought she recognized one of those voices, or perhaps two. That deep intent baying; was it Fiery? And that wild cry that spoke of wilderness and loss . . . *Yes,* thought Sweet. It was the half wolf and his Pack; she was sure of it.

I told them I wouldn't return, but I also said I wouldn't be a burden. And I won't! I'll earn my way into their Pack.

A little way down the slope, a rustling in the grass made her ears prick forward, and her body tensed. A rabbit! She licked her chops as saliva pooled in her mouth.

No dog could easily catch a rabbit alone. No *ordinary* dog. So no Alpha could fail to be impressed by a dog who could. Rabbits were so quick, so nimble, so very much faster than dogs. . . .

But not as fast as me.

The night was paling into dawn again by the time Sweet padded back into the Wild Pack territory. Her fur bristled with nerves, but her head was held high and proud, and between her jaws hung a sleek, plump rabbit.

"What in the name of the Sky-Dogs—" The deep powerful bark was full of shock, but Sweet didn't flinch. She recognized Fiery's voice, and for all his size he was a fair dog. He wouldn't kill her. Not outright, not straightaway.

Dogs were gathering around her now, some snarling, some stunned into silence, some exchanging glances of disbelief. The red Beta barged forward, butting smaller dogs aside.

"What are you doing back here, Bony Dog?" Her voice was filled with contempt. "You've just made a big mistake. And your last!"

"Wait, Beta." Fiery shoved easily through to her side, the smaller dogs moving hurriedly out of his way. "Look, she's caught a rabbit. By herself."

"That's pretty impressive." The white-and-tan dog nodded reluctantly.

"I'm certainly impressed," said a black-and-white dog who was fat with puppies. She leaned against Fiery's flank. "We could use her, Beta. There'll be more mouths to feed soon."

The red dog turned on them all, snarling. "Which means we don't need another! Our Pack has all the dogs it needs!"

"That," said a commanding voice, "is not your decision."

The half wolf Alpha stepped forward through the ranks, lashing his bushy tail as he watched Sweet's eyes. He circled her, looking her up and down till Sweet's hide began to itch. But she stayed silent.

"Look at this," he told his Pack. "Not only an impressive catch, but the strength of will to carry it here without eating it." He nudged Sweet's bony ribs with his muzzle. "And it's not as if she isn't hungry. That's the kind of discipline I like."

"You're not serious?" yelped Beta. "We know nothing about her!"

Alpha looked from his Beta back to Sweet. Thoughtfully he cocked his head.

"We know she's a good hunter," he murmured. "She's clearly respectful, and has a sense of honor. What more could we ask for in a dog?"

"I don't believe this!" snapped Beta furiously, her hackles springing up. "You can't—"

"Can't?" echoed Alpha, a dangerous edge to his silky voice. "Are you telling me I can't do something, Beta? Because it's not the first time you've questioned my authority." His growl deepened. "It's not the first time you've betrayed your delusion that *you* are Alpha here."

"No, I—"

"Do you know better than I do? Do you think you'd make a better Alpha, perhaps? Would you like to . . . *challenge* me?"

Beta ducked her head, lowering her forequarters and backing off. Sweet could not miss the flash of terror in her eyes, and no wonder. The half wolf was much bigger and more powerful than the red dog—she wouldn't stand a chance if it came to a fight.

Alpha gave a snort of dismissal, and turned back to Sweet.

"You may stay for now," he told her. "Prove yourself a valuable member of this Pack, and a loyal one"—he shot a glare at Beta—"and you can stay for good."

Murmurs of agreement went around the Pack as Sweet dipped her head in gratitude. The pregnant black-and-white dog came forward to lick her nose.

"I'm Moon. I'll show you where you'll sleep," she told Sweet cheerfully. "Welcome to our Pack!"

Sweet felt a wave of relief. *I've found a Pack. I'll howl again at the next full moon!* But she couldn't miss the glance Beta shot at her. As she turned and stalked away, the red dog's eyes glowed with resentful hatred.

CHAPTER FIVE

"Come on, Sweet. Really attack me! I know you can do this!"

Fiery barked encouragingly, lifting his head to show a tantalizing glimpse of his soft throat. Sweet, still panting for breath after her last attempt, gave him a skeptical sidelong look. Bunching her muscles, she sprang again, only for his huge paw to whack her away. She rolled into a pile of leaves and lay there, flanks heaving as she tried to gather her dignity. It was five journeys of the Sun-Dog since she'd joined this Pack, and she was no closer to besting Fiery in a training fight.

"Go on," he pleaded. "You're nearly there. Try again!"

Sweet hauled herself up onto her forepaws. It was hard enough practicing fighting techniques with a dog the size of Fiery and a hunter as nimble and lithe as Snap. But it made it a lot harder when Beta sat there smugly in the shade of a tree, scoffing under her breath at all of Sweet's feeble attempts.

Fiery was so helpful and enthusiastic, Sweet didn't have the heart to point out how wrong this all was. For a fragile and slender dog like her, Fiery's fighting strategies weren't appropriate at all, based as they were on sheer overwhelming power. Still, she hauled herself to her paws and tried again, launching herself at his shoulders and hanging grimly on.

He shook her off with a quick jerk of his massive body, and she thumped once more to the ground.

"Oh, well done, Sweetie." Beta's voice was full of sarcastic delight.

Oh, shut up, Beta, thought Sweet grimly. *You're loving this, aren't you?* Her body already ached in more places than she'd thought possible. At this rate, she wouldn't be fit even for patrolling.

"Never mind, *Sweetie,* I believe Omega can be a very fulfilling job."

Rage boiled up in Sweet's gut. With a growl of bitter resentment, she launched herself at the unprepared Fiery, seizing his scruff in her jaws, and forcing him down with the sheer weight of her fury. He was back on his paws in moments, but he shook himself and licked her in congratulation.

"Nicely done!" he barked. "See, you can do it!"

"Of course she can," agreed Snap happily.

"Huh!" Beta got to her paws and strode forward. "This is fighting practice, not mothers playing battle games with their pups! This is the Pack's survival we're talking about. I know you two feel protective, but she's useless. Those legs would break in a strong wind, for the Sky-Dogs' sake!"

Panting hard, Sweet glowered at Beta. The red dog reminded her of Callie, and the way she'd taunted and bullied Sweet in her old Pack. Beta knew just how to provoke her, just as Callie had. And Sweet couldn't help wishing for a moment that Beta would meet the same fate. . . .

No, she scolded herself. *That's not Pack thinking.* Snap and Fiery were looking away, unwilling to interfere between Sweet and their Beta. Sweet gave Beta a simpering, over-friendly, very insincere whine, just to irritate her.

The red dog glowered at her as Alpha paced over to them. "What's all the noise?" barked the half wolf.

Beta started, and gave him a nervous look. "I was giving them some fighting advice. That's all."

Alpha's face was cold and expressionless. "Interesting. I've never heard quite such *loud* advice."

"Sorry," Beta muttered, licking her chops as she backed sullenly away.

"Fiery," said Alpha sharply. "Show me what you were all working on. Then I can see what got Beta so worked up."

Fiery nudged Sweet. "Come on. Show Alpha what you can do."

Sweet took a breath, bunching her muscles in preparation for what she knew was coming. Sure enough, Fiery stretched his jaws in a grin, then sprang onto her. He knocked her flying, gripping her slender neck in his soft jaws and wrestling her to the ground.

Sweet wriggled desperately, trying to kick him off. *Come on, Sweet. Get angry again, that worked!*

The trouble was, she couldn't get angry. It was all just so *silly*. She couldn't fight like this!

Right. So I'm going to fail, in front of Alpha this time, and Beta will never let me hear the end of it. . . .

The very image of Beta's mocking sneer gave her a sudden strength. Twisting sharply, Sweet writhed out of Fiery's grip, grabbed his shoulder with her foreclaws and hauled herself on top of him. She sank her teeth into the folds of flesh at his neck, and held him down until he went limp. She had a feeling he was submitting for her benefit, so that she could impress Alpha, but she kept her teeth firmly locked on his neck. Around them, there was silence from the other dogs.

"Well," said Alpha at last, tilting his muzzle skyward. "What's wrong with that, Beta? It looks perfectly efficient to me."

"Fiery's just—" began Beta, but Alpha cut her off.

"In fact, it looks a lot sharper than some of *your* moves." The half wolf gave her a supercilious look. "I think Sweet's a natural fighter."

Despite his words, Sweet felt a twist of annoyance in her gut. What Alpha said sounded suspiciously like what the older swift-dogs used to tell her when she was a pup. *He's indulging me,* she thought angrily. *Patronizing me—just to make a point to Beta.*

Maybe Alpha was trying to boost her confidence—which would be bad enough—or maybe he was using her, to keep his Beta in her place. Whatever it was, it didn't sound honest to Sweet. She felt a growl rise in her throat, but she bit it back.

Without waiting for the stammering Beta's response, Alpha turned with a flick of his bushy tail and stalked back toward his den. Beta watched him go, then turned her ugly stare on Sweet.

"This isn't over," she snarled. She twisted and bounded into the forest.

It's not my fault! Sweet wanted to bark. Beta's hostility felt like a gigantic paw on the back of her head, shoving her down into the mud. *I didn't ask Alpha to praise me for something I didn't do!*

She knew there was no point running after Beta, though. The

red dog didn't want to listen to anything she had to say. Sweet felt a warm flank pressing against her side: Fiery. Snap too sidled closer, giving her ear a reassuring lick.

"Don't worry, Sweet," rumbled Fiery. "Alpha likes you, that's obvious. And that counts for a lot."

"Yes," agreed Snap. "And Beta had better watch her hindquarters."

Sweet took a step back, startled, and met Snap's eyes. "What do you mean?"

"Huh." Snap tilted her head and cocked a brown ear. "Every dog knows Alpha and Beta haven't been seeing eye to eye recently. Maybe you're just what's needed in this Pack to—"

"That's enough, Snap," growled Fiery sharply. "Don't gossip about your leaders. There's nothing honorable about that."

Snap gave a dismissive hunch of her shoulders, but Sweet turned to her with horror. "I don't want to cause any problems. All I wanted was a Pack, somewhere to belong. Somewhere to feel *safe*. I want to be an asset to this Pack, not make things worse!"

"That's all very well," muttered Snap, despite Fiery's warning glower. "But I'm not sure Beta's going to give you much choice. . . ."

CHAPTER SIX

With the exception of Beta, thought Sweet, her new Pack had made her life a lot happier. She felt more content now than she had since the Big Growl had struck. Already, nearly a Moon-Dog's journey after joining the Pack, she'd been elevated by Alpha to be a hunter. There was nothing more satisfying than prowling the forest for prey, doing her part to provide for the Pack. Sunlight dappled the forest floor, there was warmth in the air, and Fiery was an able and friendly hunting partner.

"Now I smell that deer you saw," said the big dog. "We're closing on it. But I'm still not sure we can catch it."

"I think we can," Sweet told him confidently. "I'm faster than it is, and I know the forest better."

When she'd first caught sight of the creature, she could tell—even from a distance—that it was not at its strongest. Many animals were underfed and scrawny, in the aftermath of the Big

Growl, but the deer would still provide a good meal for the Pack—if they could run it down.

"Deer are so easily spooked," Fiery pointed out, "and this one will be even warier. It doesn't belong in the forest, and it'll be on edge. No dog in this Pack has managed to catch one before."

"We need to drive it into the denser trees," advised Sweet. "Then it'll have far less space to dodge."

"Stop talking about it." The derisive snarl came from behind them. "Just take the deer down, or find something else."

Fiery paused to look over his shoulder. "Beta. I didn't know you were joining us."

"I'm not," growled the red dog. "I want to see how Sweetie manages a hunt."

Sweet ground her jaws together, hanging on to her temper. She knew Beta was waiting for her to fail at something—longing for it, in fact—and she'd gloat for days if Sweet failed to catch the deer now. The sneakiness of the red dog riled her so much, she could feel her muscles quiver beneath her skin—and that wouldn't help her to keep cool and calm for the hunt.

Drawing herself up, Sweet ignored Beta and turned to Fiery. "Are you ready?"

Fiery inclined his massive head. "If you think we can do it."

"I know we can." Sweet could sense Beta almost twitching with irritation. The red dog had been furious, Sweet knew, when Alpha had promoted her to hunter. If they didn't make this kill, she was certain that the tale of her failure would make its swift way to Alpha's ears. Deep in her throat, Sweet growled softly. Failure was not an option now.

"Fiery, if you circle the edge of the forest there, you'll force the deer toward me. Don't rush it, all right? Just walk in step with it; don't let it escape past you. I'll do the rest."

The big dog nodded. Without another word, to Sweet or to Beta, he padded off in a wide flanking movement. Crouching lower, watching silently, Sweet saw the deer's head come up in alarm. Taking no more notice of Beta, Sweet began to lope carefully forward.

The deer was upwind of her, and it was focused on the huge shadow of Fiery, slipping through the tree trunks to its left. It sprang forward, then hesitated, doubled back, and began to trot deeper into the trees. Again it stopped, scanning the forest, but its only concern was the threat of Fiery.

Sweet moved smoothly and silently, a lean shadow, her long legs delicately finding the best path through the leafy undergrowth.

Ahead of her the deer jerked to the side, uncertain now. Its eyes were huge.

Finally panicking, the deer leaped into a run, bolting across Sweet's path. But she was close enough now. As she sprinted to intercept it, it skidded to a halt, panicked into indecision. Sweet had only an instant, and she took it, springing and seizing the creature's throat, then hanging grimly on as Fiery plunged through the bushes to join her.

When the deer flopped limp beneath them, its kicking legs finally going still, Fiery drew back, panting. "We did it!"

"I told you we could," said Sweet quietly.

No need for noisy bragging, she thought with satisfaction. *I've proved myself to Fiery—and in front of Beta!*

Between them, she and Fiery hauled the deer's carcass back through the trees to the camp. It wasn't an easy job, thought Sweet, with her skinny legs and narrow jaws, but she had Fiery's powerful help even if she didn't have Beta's. *She disappeared fast,* thought Sweet bitterly, *when I made the kill and there was prey to drag.*

Beta continued to linger on the edges of the camp, glowering resentfully, while the rest of the Pack members gathered excitedly around the deer, barking and whining their pleasure. The dogs parted, though, when Alpha padded forward, sniffing appreciatively at the scent of dead prey.

"A fine catch." The half wolf nodded, growling with approval. "The best this Pack's ever had, in fact." He shot his contemptuous yellow gaze at Beta, still lurking on the fringes of the group, and the red dog turned and slunk into the shadows.

Sweet expected Alpha to say something to her directly, but all he did was turn on his paw and saunter back toward his den. She furrowed her brow curiously. *What is Alpha playing at?*

She had no time to worry about it, though. Fiery was busily retelling the story of the deer over and over again, to any dog who would listen.

"I tell you, I'd never have thought of it," he was saying to Snap. "Sweet was unbelievably fast. And smart!"

"I can't believe you caught an actual deer!" a young dog called Dart butted in breathlessly.

"Catch the deer? It never had a chance!" guffawed Fiery. "Not with Sweet on its tail."

"We'll have deer every day!" yelped another youngster, Twitch. "We'll never be hungry again!"

"You'll get even fatter," teased his sister, Spring.

Alpha stuck his head out of his den at that, glaring at the younger dogs. "It's a fine catch, and I said so," he growled, quieting every dog with his stare. "But don't get too comfortable. There won't always be stray deer in the forest, and even Sweet might not be able to catch them *all* the time."

He gave Sweet a cool glance that she couldn't quite read. What was that in the Alpha's yellow eyes, she wondered . . . a *challenge?* Was he trying to goad her into catching prey like that every day? Did he think she was that desperate to impress him? Sweet looked away, her fur prickling with irritation.

"How did you get to be so fast?" Spring yelped at her side.

"Yes, tell us about swift-dogs," added Dart. "How come your legs are so long and thin?"

Distracted from her annoyance with Alpha, Sweet laughed. "All right, I'll tell you where the swift-dogs came from."

Dart and Spring sat expectantly on their haunches while a few more of the Pack members gathered around. "Go on, then," said Snap, cocking an ear. "I want to hear this too."

"You've heard of the Fastest Hare?" asked Sweet, looking from dog to dog as more of the Pack sat down. "He was the worst trickster in the world. He was always playing jokes on the Spirit Dogs, and making them look like fools, and they grew very angry with him. Hares were made for dogs to chase, and no hare should get away with such insolence!

"Well, one day the Alpha of the Wind-Dogs was running through the golden meadow of the sky, and beneath her she saw the Fastest Hare keeping pace with her. As she watched him in surprise, he looked up at her and winked his yellow eye, and smirked. And then he sped up, till he was running so fast he out-paced even the Wind-Dog.

"The Alpha Wind-Dog was enraged. She went to the Sky-Dogs and demanded the Hare be punished for his impudence. So the Sky-Dogs and Wind-Dogs leaped down to the earth and sur-rounded the Hare, and demanded he put an end to his tricks. But the Hare just laughed at them, and ran between their legs, teasing them. 'I'm the Fastest Hare,' he laughed, 'and there's nothing you can do. My legs are the longest legs of all the animals, and I'm thin and narrow and I cut through the air. No one can catch me!'

"Then the Alpha Wind-Dog said, 'Sky-Dogs! You've seen for yourselves how the Hare taunts me! Give me legs that are longer than the Hare's. Give me and all my children the longest legs, and make us thin and narrow so that we cut through the air even faster than that trickster!'

"The Sky-Dogs knew that as long as the Hare had the longest

legs, he would never give them the proper respect. So they agreed to the Alpha Wind-Dog's request. They made her legs longer than the Hare's, and they made her body even thinner and narrower than his. And the next time the Hare challenged the Wind-Dog, she ran him down! She pounced, and held him in her jaws and said, 'Now you must run from me and from all my children, because we will never stop till we catch you.'

"And the Fastest Hare realized he was beaten. He begged the Alpha Wind-Dog's mercy and was humbled. From that day on, all of his children had to run from the family of the Wind-Dogs."

Sweet sat back happily, her tongue lolling, and basked in the admiring stares of the other Pack members.

"Wow," said Spring. "I haven't heard that story before."

"You haven't heard it," sneered a familiar voice, "because Sweetie made it up. There're no such Spirit Dogs as the Wind-Dogs! I've never heard such nonsense."

Sweet stared coolly at Beta as the red dog slunk into the circle. For once, her belly didn't twist with anger. *You can't provoke me now, Beta,* she thought, *any more than the Fastest Hare can taunt the Alpha Wind-Dog. I'm part of this Pack, and these dogs know it.*

Contented, she glanced around at the others, waiting for one of them to speak up, to confirm the truth of her story.

But all her Packmates did was exchange nervous glances, or stare at the forest floor. Sweet's eyes widened as the silence stretched. She shot a look at Fiery, but even he was avoiding her eyes. He licked a paw, and made a rumbling sound in his throat, and scratched his ear.

Sweet felt as if there was a stone in her belly. *It's this Pack,* she realized. *This Pack, and its rigid rules. They'll complain about how mean Beta is, but only in private. They'll never contradict her, or tell her she's wrong....*

With a heavy heart, Sweet lay down and stretched out her forepaws, pretending nonchalance, but her mind was in turmoil.

Did I make the wrong decision, joining this Pack? Was all the effort worth it?

But what was the alternative?

To be all alone in a changed, broken, empty world...

CHAPTER SEVEN

Sweet had too much time the next morning to gnaw at her worries, turning them over and over in her skull. She'd been detailed to the sunup corner of the camp and told to keep watch for a group of strange dogs, strays that had been scented but never fully seen. Alpha was so concerned, he'd told the hunters to join the patrol dogs for now, making sure the camp was fully guarded.

"We have to be particularly vigilant," Alpha had told her. "I'm relying on you, Sweet."

And she had kept a close watch on every shadow and every movement in the forest, but that didn't provide enough distraction from her worries about her place in the Pack. *Will I ever really fit in here? It's so different from my swift-dog Pack. What was that sound—a snapping twig? I wonder if Beta will ever soften her opinion of me....*

A high, agonized howl shattered Sweet's thoughts, sending

her leaping to her paws. Despite the awfulness of the sound, she recognized the voice.

Moon!

Fiery's mate must be about to give birth to her pups, Sweet realized as she raced back to the camp. *But something must be wrong for her to cry out like that—*

Sure enough, when Sweet broke out of the trees, she saw Moon lying on her flank, legs stiff and twitching, her muzzle twisted in pain. Other dogs were milling around her, looking worried, but scared to go closer.

Sweet pushed through their bodies. "Somebody has to get Fiery!" she barked.

"He's out on patrol," growled Spring nervously. "Hold on, Moon! It'll be over soon."

"He'll want to be here, especially when Moon's in pain," said Sweet urgently.

"Well, you're the fastest," Twitch pointed out. He had a lame leg himself—it had been like that since he was a pup—and he nudged it now with his muzzle, as if to point out the hopelessness of sending him.

"But I'm on guard!" Sweet looked desperately at the other dogs as Moon gave a series of yips, full of pain.

To her surprise, Beta trotted to her side. "I'll cover your area," she growled. "Twitch is right, you'll get to Fiery quickest. Go on, I'll take your place."

Sweet had no time to express her shock—or her gratitude. Beta's words made all her worries crumble away like a sandbank in a drought. If the red dog could put aside their differences for the good of all dogs, it seemed this was a true Pack after all. Sweet gave Beta a brief relieved nod, turned, and bolted out of the clearing.

Fiery's scent was not hard to pick up; when Sweet followed the usual patrol trail, she caught his odor in her nostrils straightaway. He'd been here only minutes before, she realized, leaping a fallen log and darting on. Through the next line of trees lay a broad meadow, and in the full light of the morning sun she could make out the shapes of the patrol on the low horizon. Sweet raced to catch up.

"Fiery!" she barked, her tongue lolling as she panted. "Fiery!"

The lead patrol dog turned. He must have realized it was important, because he turned and trotted rapidly back toward Sweet, and she slithered to a stop on the meadow grass, gasping.

"Moon's pup-time has come. She needs you!"

He barely hesitated. "Thank you," he growled, then bounded

off toward the forest, astonishingly fleet for such a huge dog. Sweet followed at his heels while the rest of the patrol stared after them.

Sweet caught up with Fiery as they reached the edge of the trees, though it struck her that few other dogs would have been able to match his desperate speed. She let him lead the way through the undergrowth, his bulk smashing twigs and leafy branches aside, and it seemed only moments until they reached the camp's border.

Sweet trotted to a halt, stiff-legged and shocked. Fiery stalked forward more slowly now, snarling.

Snap stood there, her back to the camp and her muzzle peeled back, facing down a pair of hungry coyotes.

"What . . . ? How in the name of the Earth-Dog did they get in?" barked Fiery, as the coyotes twisted to face the new threat.

Sweet's heart lurched. This was the section of the camp border she'd been guarding!

Fiery clearly had no time for fighting coyotes. He gave a deep, baying howl of anger, and the scrawny creatures, seeing instantly that they were outnumbered, panicked. Slipping and slithering, they almost fell over themselves as they fled the camp.

Fiery didn't give chase, but plunged straight on toward his and Moon's den, where the yaps and howls of pain were still high and frantic. Snap rounded on Sweet.

"Where were you?" she barked.

Sweet licked her chops, confused and afraid. "I—I had to fetch Fiery! I thought Beta was patrolling this area! She said—she told me she'd cover for me." Her ears drooped as her breathing calmed at last. "Something must have happened. She must have been called away, Snap. I—"

"Oh, don't worry," grunted Snap through clenched jaws. She was still getting her own breath back after the panic. "No harm done, in the end. Just as well I was here, though. With Alpha away on patrol, and everyone distracted by Moon's pup-time."

"How is she?" begged Sweet, craning her head to peer toward the noise from Moon's den.

"I don't know." Snap glanced grimly over her shoulder. "There's obviously a problem. She was in pain, and—ah!"

The sudden quietness was oppressive. Snap and Sweet stared at each other, and Sweet knew the hunt-dog felt the same sudden, awful fear as she did.

Then Fiery broke the silence with a howl of joy. His deep voice was joined by Moon's, feebler, but filled with relief and happiness.

Snap's ears pricked up. "The pups. They're born!"

She turned, and she and Sweet bounded toward the den

together. As they reached it, Fiery was just emerging, the strain on his blunt face still visible through the pride and pleasure.

"Three fine pups," he announced gruffly. "Two males and a female!"

"Congratulations."

The drawling voice made every dog turn, as Alpha padded toward the den, his ears pricked in mild curiosity.

"Thank you, Alpha," Fiery dipped his head respectfully, but his tail still wagged with irrepressible happiness.

"Three fine pups? That's good news for the Pack." That seemed to be the extent of Alpha's interest, though, because he turned to Sweet and Snap, his face becoming grim. "You two, and Beta . . . come with me."

Her stomach heavy with foreboding, Sweet followed him, together with Snap and Beta. A rabbit-chase from the other dogs, Alpha turned and sat on his haunches, then stared at them each in turn.

"How did coyotes get into this camp?" he asked. His tone was too quiet, too calm.

Sweet opened her jaws to explain, but again Beta was too fast for her. "They got in from that direction," said the red dog, jerking her muzzle toward Sweet's patrol zone. "*She* was supposed to be guarding that spot, I think?"

"I went to find Fiery!" Sweet looked desperately from Beta's sly face to Alpha's. "We all—the dogs who were here agreed that Moon needed her mate. I was the fastest!"

"That's no reason to abandon your post!" snapped Alpha.

"But I didn't! Beta said she'd cover for me!"

"Liar." Beta's low snarl made Sweet's blood run cold. "I haven't seen you all day."

Sweet opened her jaws, but no sound would come out. Of course, if Beta had been lured away somehow—if she'd been distracted enough to allow the coyotes to breach their boundaries—she would want to play down her own mistake. But did she have to lie and blame everything on Sweet? Sweet's nerves prickled with fear and disbelief.

They'll think I ran away—again. . . . It's happening again! I'm the Dog Who Ran Away. . . .

"But I didn't!" she barked out loud in panic. "I didn't run away!"

"You two." Alpha glared at Snap and Beta. "Leave us."

Snap shot Sweet a sympathetic look, but Beta's eyes were cunning and vindictive as she slunk away. Sweet swallowed hard as their pawsteps faded into the trees. Then she turned, skin quivering, to face Alpha. His stern yellow stare was unnerving.

"You're putting me in a very difficult position, Sweet," he growled softly. "Making these puppish errors."

"I'm sorry, Alpha. I misunderstood. I thought that Beta—"

"You're just getting used to Wild Pack life. . . ." He interrupted as if she hadn't spoken. "So I have to make allowances. I won't punish you as you should be punished. Not this time."

Sweet dipped her head. It was probably best to keep silent, she decided, though confusion and anger stirred in her gut.

"Next time, you'll find I'm not so understanding," he growled silkily. "Tonight you'll be on watch from dusk till sunup; I don't care how tired you are. You *will* protect this Pack throughout the no-sun hours. Perhaps that will teach you Pack discipline."

Sweet watched the half wolf as he stalked away toward his den. A sense of injustice roiled in her belly, but there was something else, too.

She knew Alpha expected her to be grateful for his mercy, but she wasn't. All she felt was resentment, and a deep, gnawing suspicion.

The half wolf was up to something; she knew it.

* * *

In the darkness of the wild wood, later that night, Sweet lay with her head on her paws and gazed up at the Moon-Dog. Her huge eye was full and bright in the sky again, reminding Sweet that she'd been with this Pack now for a full Moon-Dog journey.

And now, for the first Great Howl since she'd joined them, she was exiled to the camp's edges, her punishment for letting those coyotes sneak in. Through the trees she could hear the first voices rise, then others as they joined in harmony. The Howl swelled and rose, making the night air quiver, and raising Sweet's fur at the roots.

It felt strange. Despite her isolation out here, she didn't feel lonely, as she had when as an outsider she'd first heard their distant howling. Even though she wasn't with them right now, she felt the connection in her bones and her blood: a living, thrilling link to her Pack, and this forest, and the wounded earth they walked on.

The wounded earth that never howled, that clenched its fangs against the pain it must feel at being torn apart . . .

Sitting up, Sweet tilted her head back. Unable to repress it, she let the howl grow in her belly and her throat, swelling until the cry of emotion escaped her. Even if she wasn't among them, she could howl with her Pack, she could join her voice and her whole being to theirs.

The sensation of belonging filled Sweet as if it was a second stream of blood in her veins. With that knowledge came a deep feeling of peace. Beta couldn't touch that, not deep down; and even Alpha couldn't affect it with his tricks and manipulations. Her connection was with the Pack and its spirit, and only she could break it.

And I'd never want to. After all the times she'd run away—from the Trap House, from Lucky, from her first swift-dog Pack—she found suddenly that the urge to run was gone.

This was where she belonged—this land, this forest, this Pack.

CHAPTER EIGHT

The high of the Great Howl couldn't last forever, and Sweet was exhausted and aching from her long watch by the time the sky began to pale where the Sun-Dog would rise. Her leg muscles ached from the fast sprint to find Fiery, and her mind felt stunned by the Howl itself, but its message had lodged firmly inside her heart and guts. She wouldn't let her Pack down now. She'd defend their home against anything.

If she truly had abandoned her post, she mused, she'd have earned this punishment, and worse. She still wondered if perhaps Alpha knew more about that than he was letting on. Did he in fact know why no dog was there to stop the coyotes? Did he know what had really happened? And if so, why had he gone through with this?

She didn't trust the half wolf, Sweet admitted inwardly. *But I'm not at all sure why. . . .*

A branch cracked behind her, and she leaped to her feet, hackles high; but instantly she recognized the two dogs. Fiery was unmistakable, with his square head and his massive body, and Moon's white-and-black coat gleamed in the early dawn. The new mother dog leaned weakly against her mate's flank, but as they drew closer to Sweet she left Fiery's side to lick Sweet's ear and nuzzle her neck.

"Thank you for what you did, Sweet," murmured Moon. "I'm so sorry it got you into trouble. But Fiery came to me in time to see the last of his pups born. I don't know if I'd have had the strength, otherwise."

"I can't thank you enough," rumbled Fiery. The sire-pride in his eyes looked as if it would never dim. "Our pups don't have names yet, but one day soon they will—and I hope they grow up to be as loyal and brave as you, Sweet."

The two dogs' words made Sweet's gut twist and her heart warm with gratitude. She returned their fond licks. "Thank you. Both of you. I'm only glad I could help."

"You helped more than we can say," Moon told her. "And you didn't deserve this punishment. We both know you'd never have left your post and abandoned the camp." She took a breath, as if to say more, then shut her jaws.

"We have to go back to the pups," said Fiery softly, nuzzling his mate. "But remember what we owe you, Sweet. Because *we* won't forget."

Sweet watched them go, vanishing into the shadows. The warmth inside her was kindling to a fierce glow of protectiveness.

No. I'll never let my friends down again.

Just as the Sun-Dog was rising, his light glinting fiercely through the trees, Fiery returned, relieving Sweet of her watch and telling her kindly but firmly to get some sleep. Gratefully Sweet accepted, slinking exhaustedly back into the camp. Her eyes and ears drooped and her paws felt like boulders, but it seemed she wasn't to get any sleep just yet. Alpha was summoning the Pack into the clearing, his tail tapping impatiently on the rock where he sat.

As he caught sight of her approaching, he gave a low bark, and every dog turned, pricking their ears.

"Hear this, dogs of my Pack. Sweet's punishment is over. She is forgiven her error and she will rejoin the hunting dogs today."

Just behind him there was a low snarl, and Alpha half turned. Beta stood there, her muscles trembling with anger and her hackles bristling.

SURVIVORS: SWEET'S JOURNEY

Alpha said nothing. He kept his yellow stare level on Beta till she was forced to meet it. The red dog's tail lowered, and she fell silent.

"That's settled, then," growled Alpha. "Every dog, go to your duties. Sweet, get some sleep. You'll need it before you hunt."

Without the refreshment of a brief sleep, Sweet didn't think she'd have managed to catch any prey at all. The hunt that day was long and hard, and as she returned to her den afterward, she felt hunger gnaw at her belly; the sting of it reminded her that she hadn't eaten anything since before her long night's guard duty. But the ache in her muscles was a good one. She was a part of the team again, a good and hardworking dog, a valuable member of the Pack.

She stopped at the entrance to her den and sniffed. *Food?*

Happiness made her light-headed. Fiery and Moon had left her a rabbit from the Pack's earlier meal. *It's good to have a Pack,* she thought. *It's good to have friends.*

She could barely even wait to give thanks to the Forest-Dog. Falling on the rabbit, she pinned it with her forepaws and began to tear at it, gulping chunks of it down. The feeling of warm food in her empty belly was bliss, chasing away all the fears and worries and sadness of the night before. For long, ravenous moments, Sweet didn't even see the shadow that fell across her.

Only when Beta's howl rang out above her did she jerk her head up, startled.

"Sweet has eaten the common prey! She has deprived the Pack and its pups, and filled her own belly!"

Sweet stared up at the red dog, her jaw loose, dizzy for an instant with disbelief and bewilderment. *What?*

Then, as she caught the vicious glint in Beta's eyes, she realized. *Beta left this rabbit here! It was Beta!*

Sweet shuffled hastily back from the torn prey, but she knew it was too late. Her mouth was bloody and stained, and still full of rabbit meat.

She could only crouch, trembling, on the ground as Alpha stalked toward her, followed by her Packmates. The taste of the meat in her jaws was like acrid dust; she couldn't even swallow it.

"Sweet." Alpha's bark was thunderous. "This is the worst offense a Pack member can commit."

"Alpha, I—" Her whine was so hoarse, she could barely hear it herself.

"If you really did this, Sweet," Alpha growled, "you will be scarred both as punishment and as a sign to every dog of what you are. What do you have to say for yourself? How do you respond to Beta's charge?"

The half wolf's yellow eyes were entirely unreadable. Sweet stared into them, transfixed with horror, searching for a trace of pity, or a trace of doubt.

I won't be scarred for something I didn't do. I will not let it happen!

But how can I stop it? I have no witnesses to speak for me! Beta planned this, she planned it perfectly from the start. . . .

She could spring to her paws right now, she thought, turn and run. No dog here could catch her if she was determined. She was the fastest of all of them.

But then she could never come back. *Never.* Finally tearing her eyes away from Alpha's, she met Fiery's steady clear gaze.

Fiery wants me to deny it. He wants me to prove myself—he wants to know he and Moon were right to trust me. . . .

Something churned in Sweet's belly, and a spark of fire flared in her heart.

I will not be the Dog Who Runs. Not this time. I will be the Dog Who Stands Her Ground.

Sweet raised herself to her paws. She stood foursquare, her legs so rigid she was afraid they would tremble. But she gazed once more, this time with defiance, into Alpha's eyes.

"Alpha. Dogs of my Pack," she barked, and her voice rang out clear and strong. "I reject Beta's charge. She is lying. I will prove myself, here and now, in combat."

She turned to the red dog, and gazed at her icily.

"*I challenge Beta.*"

CHAPTER NINE

The air in the camp crackled with tension, lifting the roots of Sweet's fur. Dogs were drawing back into a wide circle, their eyes wide and their ears pricked in nervous expectation. There were small whines of anxiety, and a few excited growls of anticipation, quickly stifled.

Sweet kept her eyes on Beta, who stood rigid, as if in shock. The red dog's jaws were slightly parted, but as Sweet watched, she recovered, and her lips stretched in a sneer over her sharp fangs.

At Sweet's side, Moon murmured, "Is this what you wanted all along, Sweet? To challenge Beta and become Alpha's second in command?"

Sweet cocked one ear at her friend. "Of course not. That has nothing to do with this." She frowned. "I'm tired of putting up with her, that's all. Taunting me, playing tricks. The Wind-Dogs wouldn't put up with it from the Hare. If I tolerated it from Beta,

I'd be letting down Alpha Wind-Dog herself!" A fierce thrill of determination went down Sweet's spine as she said it. *Wind-Dogs,* she thought, *be with me! Give me the speed I need!*

"Hear me, dogs of my Pack," barked Alpha. "Sweet the swift-dog challenges Beta." He glanced around them all, then stepped back and nodded to the two challengers.

"Be careful, Sweet," Moon whispered, licking her ear. "Beta is a good and clever fighter. And she's ruthless."

"I know she is." Sweet nodded calmly. "But I can either stand up to her, or I can run. And I won't be the Dog Who Runs, not anymore. I've tried that, and I always regret it. Now, I'm going to be the Dog Who Stands."

"You'll stand," snarled Beta, "till I grind you into the dust." She flung herself at Sweet, fangs snapping, claws lashing.

Sweet whirled, ducked, and flew beneath Beta's charging body. If Beta had hoped to catch her off guard with a single violent charge, thought Sweet, she was wrong. She twisted, raking her claws at Beta's underbelly as the red dog tumbled and rolled off-balance.

Sweet missed, but Beta had not laid a claw on her, either. Furious, Beta sprang back to her paws and charged again. This time Sweet's haunches were bunched beneath her and she propelled herself upward so that Beta skidded in the dust, missing again. But Beta was fast, too, and one of her flailing paws caught Sweet's flank, drawing blood.

Sweet scrabbled to a stop, turning quickly to face her enemy. She could feel blood beading on her flank, and the warm trickle as it began to flow. She clenched her jaws.

"You're pathetic, Bony Dog," snarled Beta.

Sweet resisted the temptation to return insult for insult. She was faster than Beta, but she was going to need all her breath and all her wits to stay out of reach of those savage claws. She dodged sideways again as Beta lunged, feeling sharp teeth graze her leg, but she'd escaped once more without a deep wound. As Beta stumbled, Sweet snapped her long muzzle at the red dog's hind leg. Her jaws closed satisfyingly on flesh and bone, and Beta yelped. Sweet released her, and sprang back out of reach.

Both dogs stood rigid, eyeing each other, panting hard. Around them there was silence from the rest of the Pack; Sweet didn't hear so much as a whine or a quiet yelp.

Beta began to circle again, and Sweet turned slowly, watching her.

This time, Beta's attack was still powerful, but she took more care, and Sweet darted forward to meet her, teeth bared. Beta dodged her bite, and swiped her claws at Sweet's eyes, one claw nicking her cheekbone. Sweet gave a yelp of anger.

She's fighting like Callie used to. Aiming for my eyes! She doesn't care if she blinds me—she'd rather kill me than see me part of this Pack!

The realization sent new strength and determination flowing into Sweet's blood. *This is one fight I won't lose.*

Beta's moves were slyer now, more considered, but Sweet could see the red light of fury in her blazing eyes. *She's not in complete control of herself. If I can tempt her in closer —*

Sweet bounded forward, head twisting as if to bite. Beta lunged for her eyes again, but this time Sweet ducked and rolled. Beta's forepaw slammed into the dust beside her head, and Sweet took her chance. She snapped for the red dog's foreleg, seizing it between her jaws and crunching down hard. Through the pounding of blood in her ears, she heard Beta's screaming howl of pain.

I can't give her a single chance. Sweet twisted up onto her forepaws, Beta's leg still clamped in her teeth, and yanked hard. Her teeth tore into the flesh, and against the soft inside of her mouth she felt something strain and snap in her enemy's leg muscles.

Beta's howl turned into a shrieking yelp. Her big body collapsed sideways, thumping into the dust. Sweet flung herself on top of the red dog, releasing her leg and grabbing a tight hold on her neck.

"Yield!" she snarled through a mouthful of fur and flesh. "*Yield!*"

Beta was squirming and wriggling and whining with fury beneath her, but Sweet had her pinned. At last, flanks heaving, the red dog went limp, her teeth still bared in a snarl.

"I . . . I *yield*."

Sweet left her teeth in Beta's scruff a moment longer, to make certain, then abruptly released her. She scrambled off the red dog's sprawled body, letting her stagger to her paws and stand there, panting with defeated fury.

Sweet lifted her head high. "You made me out to be a thief, Beta. You called me a food-stealer and a deserter in front of my Pack." Her fangs clenched. "You lied."

Beta's tail was low and her head hung down, but her face still wore its hateful snarl.

"You lied, Beta," barked Sweet in her face. "Say it!"

"I lied," growled Beta, "to rid our Pack of a useless lightweight."

Sweet's muzzle curled, but she didn't respond. She didn't have to. All around, other dogs were muttering, growling, barking out the things they hadn't dared say before.

"Beta did lie. I never believed Sweet would steal," whined Twitch.

"Not after she carried that rabbit all the way here," barked Spring in agreement.

"Beta's sneaky that way," growled Snap. "I always said you couldn't trust her."

Fiery gave Snap a sidelong frown of disapproval, but he said, "You can trust Sweet."

"Yes," said Moon, coming forward to lick the swift-dog's ear. "Sweet has always been a good dog. She's an asset to this Pack."

Sweet glanced at Beta. She almost felt sorry for her, but she couldn't afford to give in to pity. Beta had pushed and pushed till Sweet had had no choice, and Sweet knew that she couldn't show weakness now. That was the world after the Big Growl: it was about survival. And she would survive. She knew now that she had the strength.

Beta curled her muzzle as she regained her breath and her dignity. "Enjoy your victory, Sweet." She didn't call her *Sweetie* now, thought Sweet with satisfaction. "But you just wait. I'll challenge you again, swift-dog. I'll challenge you on a day when I'm not tired from hunting, and I'll take back my rightful place in this Pack."

"No," came a silky voice. "No, you won't."

SURVIVORS: SWEET'S JOURNEY

Alpha paced forward as dogs gave way before him, drawing back, every eye riveted on him. He stalked right up to Beta, till his nose was almost touching hers. Silence fell among the other Pack members.

"You lost this challenge, Beta," he growled. "Not that *Beta* is your name anymore. But you lost more than a fight, and you know it. You've been exposed as a liar and a traitor, and this Pack has no room for dishonorable dogs. Leave now."

Beta looked stunned. Her jaws parted. At last she stammered, "But, Alpha—"

"Leave," he snarled. "Leave now, *Packless dog,* while you still can."

There was no mistaking the threat in his voice. Beta could only stare at him, her face stricken. She took a pace backward, glancing to left and right, and her gaze fell on Sweet.

The hatred there was piercing, but at least it was fleeting. With a heartbroken whine, Beta turned and limped away into the forest.

Sweet shook off the tremor that rippled through her skin. *I can't help thinking I haven't seen the last of her. . . .*

For now, though, life with the Pack promised to be a lot more peaceful, she thought with relief. The Pack was dispersing, and dogs were murmuring and gossiping about the unexpected turn of events. Only Alpha still stood there, watching her with his head slightly cocked.

"Well, Sweet," he growled. "Are you ready for this? You are Beta of this Pack now."

Sweet raised her head, slightly shocked. "Alpha, that's not why I fought her. I know that's the rule, but I never really wanted—I mean, I only wanted to challenge her lies, stop her bullying me . . ."

The half wolf hunched his shoulders, looking amused. "Whether you meant it or not, Sweet, you can't break Pack rules. You defeated our Beta in a lawful challenge."

Sweet stared at him, her jaws slightly parted. It made sense, and Moon had warned her, but it really hadn't crossed her mind when she issued her challenge to the red dog. *Maybe,* she thought, *I didn't quite think this through. . . .*

The light in Alpha's eyes was somewhere between mirth and menace.

"You'd better get used to it, swift-dog. You are now the Beta of this Pack."

CHAPTER TEN

How in the name of the Earth-Dog, thought Sweet, *could I ever have hesitated? How could I have thought I wouldn't get used to being Beta?*

She bounded ahead to where Spring and Dart were tugging at a deer's leg, straining to drag it back to camp. Still gripping with their teeth, they both looked up at her, cocking their ears, waiting for her orders.

"Pull to the left, there," she barked encouragingly. "There's a tussock, see? The haunches are getting caught on it. You'll have to drag it around." She seized the deer's neck in her own jaws and began to tug on it, showing them the way. Both the other dogs squatted back on their haunches, using the leverage to drag the deer's body farther.

"Thanks for coming out here to help us, Beta." Dart let go of the deer for a moment, panting. "This prey's awkward, to say the least."

"But you brought it down," Sweet pointed out encouragingly.

Dart's jaws broadened in a grin. "Yes. I never thought we'd manage one, but your training tips were exactly right. We don't all have to be fast, so long as we have enough hunters to drive it."

"Even Twitch contributed," said Spring, sounding proud of her litter-brother. "That leg holds him back, but he followed your advice and stayed out to the flank. If he hadn't been in position, the deer would have gotten away."

Sweet felt warm with pleasure and satisfaction. "I'm glad the training paid off," she said.

"We're going to do some more sparring this evening, before prey-sharing, aren't we?" Dart twitched an ear hopefully. "I'd like to learn some of your speed-tricks for a fight."

"I need to organize tomorrow's patrols," said Sweet cautiously. "Moon's still excused from hunting duty because of her pups, so we're shortpawed. But after that, why not?" She gave Dart's ear an affectionate flick of her tongue. "I've learned a lot from the Pack, so if there's anything I can teach you back, I'm happy."

"I love learning new fighting skills," said Dart. "It's been

SURVIVORS: SWEET'S JOURNEY

a long time since the Pack freshened up our tactics. You know Alpha, he does nothing about that or hunting practice, just skulks in his den all—"

"*Dart*," growled Spring warningly.

Sweet shot her a dry look—Spring was one of the dogs who'd had her ears nipped by Fiery for bad-mouthing the old Beta—but on this occasion the young dog was right. Dart really shouldn't show disrespect to Alpha. It was true that he took little part in organizing patrols, or training the younger dogs, but that was fine by Sweet. She enjoyed being Beta more than she'd ever expected, and she was happy to take on the half wolf's share of the practical work. After all, she was rewarded with the second-best choice of prey at the end of the day, and she never went hungry or grew thin from hard work. And in her more fanciful moments, she could imagine she was in charge of the whole Pack herself—that *she* was Alpha.

I should have stood up to the old Beta sooner, she thought ruefully. *For that matter, I should have faced down Callie long ago, in the days when I was still in my old Pack. She'd probably have respected me more if I had.*

And I'm good at this, better than I ever knew. If I'd been Beta of the swift-dog Pack, maybe we would never have been caught by the longpaws. Maybe then so many of us wouldn't have died in that terrible Trap House. . . .

The dogs had dragged the deer almost to the edge of the camp by now, and Sweet was distracted from her regrets when a small squirming body bumped into her paw. A tiny pup, its eyes still blurry, had escaped from Moon's den and was wobbling its way into the outside world.

"You're an adventurous one." Laughing, Sweet left Dart and Spring to haul the deer by themselves to the prey pile. She picked up the tiny pup gently in her mouth and carried it back to Moon, ignoring its protesting squeaks.

Moon appeared at the entrance to the den, her face anxious, but when she caught sight of Sweet, her jaws relaxed and she let her tongue loll. She sat down and woofed gently to her pup.

"Oh, Squirm! You're such a wanderer already, little one!"

Sweet set the tiny pup down. As soon as he smelled his mother, he blundered under her body and nestled there, clearly deciding adventure could wait till he was a few hours older.

"Another good hunt, Sweet?" Moon nuzzled her shoulder. "The Pack's been well-fed this last Moon-Dog journey. I think you've brought us good luck."

"I hope so. I owe you all so much." Sweet returned Moon's affectionate lick. "The pups are looking healthy!"

"They're already getting too lively—oh!" Moon snapped her

head around to stare, and Sweet stiffened, her hackles springing erect.

The peace of the evening and the relaxed mood were shattered as Snap bounded into the clearing, her volley of barks sharp and urgent.

"Dogs! Dogs are approaching. A strange Pack! In our territory!"

Now Sweet saw why Alpha was the head of the Pack. He sprang out of his den, leaped up to his favorite boulder and let loose a deep, barking howl of summons.

"Packmates! Our territory is threatened by strangers. Prepare for battle!"

Instantly Snap, Spring, Dart, Twitch, and Fiery bounded to his side, tails high and ears pricked keenly forward. Alpha barked out orders, fast and confident, and in moments he was tearing into the woods, his loyal followers at his heels.

Filled with true admiration for her leader for the first time, Sweet paused only for a moment. After checking over the camp to make sure Moon and her pups were safe and well defended, she left them with a reassuring bark, and followed the rest of the fighting party.

I've never been in a real battle before, she thought. *Only food-fights with other Packs, and the fight with the longpaws—and I ran away from that.*

Well, Sweet wasn't running from this battle. She was actually running toward it—and not only was she determined, she felt a thrill of real excitement in her skin and blood and nerves. She was the Beta of a powerful Wild Pack, and she was running to confront its enemies.

The others were just ahead of her now, racing up a dry streambed, leaping from rock to flat rock, with Alpha in the lead. Sweet bounded forward to lope alongside at his flank, her muscles tingling with pride. Alpha slowed as he reached a ridge, then turned and ran along below the skyline till he reached a tumble of sandstone boulders. He trotted silently among them and halted, glaring down into the shallow valley below.

At his side, Sweet panted quietly as she watched the ragtag bunch of dogs who were trotting down the valley. She narrowed her eyes in surprise.

It was the oddest Pack she'd ever seen. There was a black, shaggy dog who was massive, but did not look particularly fierce. At her side were two stocky little dogs, one with a snub nose, and one with a pointed face. There was a black-and-white farm dog who kept retracing his steps and herding the others, fussing over them and trying to keep them together. There was a yellow-coated dog who reminded Sweet, a little painfully, of Lucky the City Dog—but this was a female, her fur sleeker and shorter, and she didn't move with Lucky's strutting, jaunty confidence. The last was an extraordinary-looking animal, and for a moment Sweet wasn't sure it was a dog at all. It looked like a trailing bundle of white moss, except that it had tiny eyes in front, and a black button-nose. It gave a pathetic little yelp as a strand of its fur caught on a branch.

A low growl was building in Alpha's throat, and Sweet shook herself. No matter how bizarre this Pack of mutts looked, they were still intruders. And they must be more dangerous than they looked—because why else would they trot so confidently into the territory of a half wolf like Alpha?

"Take them down," snarled Alpha.

Sweet gave him a nod, then growled low in her throat to summon the others into their fighting positions.

"Ready?" she snarled. "Let's teach these mutts to stay out of our Pack-lands."

The others growled their angry agreement, and Sweet bounded forward, racing down the hill. The intruder dogs didn't even notice them at first, and when their heads at last came up, there was nothing but stupid shock on their blank faces.

Alpha was behind her. "Draw blood," he howled. "Drive them away!"

Sweet hurtled into battle, knocking one of the small dogs off its paws and sending it tumbling, stunned and winded. But even as she spun to snap at another, something caught the corner of her vision.

There was something in the trees, higher up the valley.

She paused, just for a moment, her fangs still bared. Was she seeing things?

Probably.

Sweet lashed out with her claws, focusing on the fight, but the strange dogs were already spinning, panicked, trying to flee.

She glanced up the valley's slope once more. Because she was sure, now, that she hadn't imagined it.

That flash of movement—it had been no lazy, street-dog strut. It was an animal, charging from between the trees, strong legs pounding in desperation.

And the Sun-Dog's light gleamed on shaggy, golden fur. . . .

MOON'S CHOICE

PACK LIST

MOON'S PACK

ALPHA:

black-and-white male Farm Dog (Moon's Father-Dog)

BETA:

black-and-white female Farm Dog (Moon's Mother-Dog)

HUNTERS:

HUNTER—big gray-and-brown male dog

RUSH—golden brown short-haired male terrier with a short tail

MEADOW—small beige female terrier with dark ears

FLY—brown-and-white, snub-nosed male dog with long legs

PATROL DOGS:

MOON—black-and-white female Farm Dog

SNAP—small female with tan-and-white fur

MULCH—black long-haired male with long ears

PEBBLE—young black female dog with sleek fur

STAR—black-and-white female Farm Dog, Moon's littermate

OMEGA:

> small, black, oddly shaped male with tiny ears and a wrinkled face (also known as Whine)

WILD PACK

ALPHA:

> huge half wolf with gray-and-white fur and yellow eyes

BETA:

> female red dog with long ears and a feathery tail

HUNTERS:

> **FIERY**—massive brown-and-black male with long ears and shaggy fur

> **SPRING**—female tan chase-dog with black patches

PATROL DOGS:

> **DART**—lean brown-and-white female chase-dog

> **TWITCH**—male tan chase-dog with black patches and a lame foot

CHAPTER ONE

A *soft blue-gray mist hung on* the horizon, but the sky above the young dog was clear as it dimmed toward night. Moon watched her namesake Spirit Dog stretch and lope into view. The Moon-Dog was half in shadow, but still she shone bright enough to make a dog mistake the dusk for daylight. A whine of anticipation rose in Moon's throat as she gazed up at her.

Just now the Pack members were going about their last duties of the day: Snap and Mulch were checking the border where a protective thornbush had blown down in the last storm; Whine, the little Omega, was trotting from den to den, renewing the bedding of the more senior dogs. Night had almost fallen, and soon the hunt patrol would return to camp, and the Pack would eat together. Then there might be time to lie contentedly, with a full belly, and talk about the day to her Mother-Dog and Father-Dog.

Moon could hear the two of them behind her in the den,

discussing some serious issue about Pack life in low voices. Moon knew that as Alpha and Beta of the Pack, her parent-dogs' duties came first; it would be the same for her, when her time came to be Pack leader. She had to be patient.

She had to be more patient than Star, anyway, she thought with a roll of her blue eyes. Her litter-sister kept bounding up to her, backing off, thrashing her tail, and snapping playfully. She was desperate to entice Moon into a fight-game, but Moon was having none of it. Fight-games were for pups!

"Star, settle down!" she yipped, swiping a gentle paw at her litter-sister's ear.

Star rolled over, pawing the air, snapping at a moth. "Oh, Moon, have some fun while you still can. You won't have any time to play at *all* once you're Alpha!"

"We're both too old to be playing," Moon told her firmly.

Star scrabbled back upright, sat down, and scratched at one ear. "You're no fun anymore," she said, an edge in her voice.

Moon pinned her ears back, surprised. She had never heard Star sound quite so resentful before. *That's not true! It's just that I'm going to have responsibilities one day. I'll need to be ready for them. . . .*

She found that her litter-sister's accusation stung, more than she'd expected. It wasn't that Star was jealous of Moon's destiny as the next Pack-Alpha; Star had no interest in the hard work and duties that would come with leadership, and Moon knew she was happy to be a free spirit. But surely Star realized, now that they were both older, that Moon didn't have the same liberty to mess around and play pointless games, didn't she?

I must learn to be serious and dutiful.

Before she could gnaw at her anxiety any longer, a new sound made Moon's ears prick up. Those were pawsteps, coming toward the camp through the undergrowth—yes, the hunt patrol was returning! The hunt-dogs' shapes became recognizable as they drew closer and emerged from the bushes: Rush and Meadow, the wily terriers; Fly, the brown-and-white snub-nosed dog with the sad but watchful eyes; and in the lead, biggest and strongest of all, was Hunter. Moon felt her heart skip a nervous beat as Hunter's eyes caught hers. He lifted his head slightly with pride; between his strong jaws was a plump and good-sized rabbit.

Moon rose to her paws, ignoring Star's snort of amusement. She dipped her head in solemn greeting, and Hunter gave a low whine of reply in his throat.

He's so well-named, she thought. *He's the strongest dog in the Pack, besides my Father-Dog, and he's the best hunter. I'm glad my parent-dogs chose him for me.*

She sometimes wondered what it was going to be like, running the Pack with Hunter as her Beta. It couldn't be anything but exciting, she decided, with a warm rush of gladness. She ignored the prickle of tension in her neck fur; nervousness and uncertainty were silly. She would be lucky to have such a strong and capable mate. Her parent-dogs had chosen carefully, and they were never wrong about such important Pack matters.

She would go on making her Father-Dog and Mother-Dog proud, and she'd go on showing her gratitude to them and her favor to Hunter. *I don't care what Star thinks about it,* Moon decided a little grumpily. It was true that she didn't feel completely comfortable in Hunter's company—he wasn't the easiest dog to talk to, and he had a stern taciturnity that sometimes bordered on sullenness—but in time, they'd learn to get along. Why, she felt guilty for thinking even the mildest criticism of him; it felt like disloyalty to her parent-dogs. She and Hunter would make a perfect match in the end, she knew it.

Behind Moon, the fir branches rustled as her Father-Dog emerged from the den and shook his fur. He waited expectantly as Hunter padded up to him and dropped the fat rabbit at his forepaws.

"Well done, Hunter! Your day was good, then?"

"It was, Alpha," replied Hunter, lashing his tail from side to side. "Plentiful prey, though some of it was too fast for the rest of the patrol."

It wasn't the first time she'd heard Hunter criticize other dogs in his hunting patrol, but on this occasion Moon was a little startled. Rush and Meadow were very capable stalkers, after all, and long-legged Fly was a swift and agile runner. But as she glanced toward the brown-and-white dog limping up behind Hunter, she noticed he did look stiff and tired. He placed his paws awkwardly, as if he was trying not to stumble, and his eyes seemed much duller than usual.

"Still, you've all done a fine job," Moon's Father-Dog was saying. He didn't seem to have noticed the change in Fly's condition; he was too busy admiring Hunter's rabbit. "The Pack will eat well tonight."

Hunter gave his Alpha a nod of acknowledgment and stepped back, his eyes still shining with pride in his catch, but Moon nudged her litter-sister with her shoulder.

"Fly doesn't look well," she whispered to Star. "Don't you think?"

Star cocked her head, frowning at Fly. He was sitting on his haunches now, his noble head drooping. His lolling tongue looked dry and swollen.

"It was a long hunt," Star muttered uneasily, "so he's probably just tired. And hungry—he'll feel better when we've all eaten."

Moon wasn't so sure, but she put Fly out of her head for the moment as the Pack began to gather for prey-sharing. Alpha and Beta, as was their right, claimed the first share, taking Hunter's rabbit between them, but there was plenty of other prey for the rest of the dogs. As soon as his leaders had eaten their fill, Hunter paced forward and selected a juicy squirrel for himself. Moon could forgive the arrogant tilt of his head, the aura of satisfaction that surrounded him. After all, he'd done more than any dog to provide this feast. She watched him brightly and approvingly, ignoring any unease she felt at his cockiness.

He's my future mate. It's good that he's strong and confident!

She felt Star's breath at her ear. "Look at him," her litter-sister muttered. "Thinks his tail touches the Sky-Dogs. Do you really want to be mated with him?"

It irritated Moon that Star could reawaken all her own uncertainties with a well-placed jibe. "It doesn't matter," she growled quietly. "The Pack needs strong leaders, and that's what Hunter is."

Star licked her chops and lay down with a sigh, clearly deciding the best policy was to keep her jaws shut. Moon was glad. She could feel her hackles bristling, yet she knew she shouldn't let Star's words ruffle her fur. Her sister was talking nonsense, obviously.

All the same, she couldn't help stealing a glance at her parent-dogs. Now that they'd eaten, and their daily responsibilities were behind them for another night, they were chuffing quietly together over some unheard joke. Alpha muttered something in Beta's ear, and in playful impatience she batted his nose with a gentle paw.

They had such a connection, thought Moon wistfully. Her Father-Dog and her Mother-Dog were friends as well as mates, companions as well as leaders. They respected each other, worked well together . . .

Against her will, the inner voice and its doubts rose inside her head. Moon clenched her jaws and rubbed her paws over her ears.

If I wasn't destined to be the Pack's Alpha . . . would I choose Hunter at all?

CHAPTER TWO

Fly's den was cool, sheltered from the Sun-Dog's rays by overhanging boughs of pine, but the big brown-and-white dog lay listlessly, panting as if the heat was unbearable. Moon nuzzled his dry nose, anxious. His flanks looked hollow and his coat was dull. A crusty discharge oozed from his exhausted eyes.

"Here," she said, trying to sound cheerful as she carefully dragged a curved piece of bark close to his muzzle. Water shimmered in it, cool and enticing, but Fly's nose barely twitched. "I brought you this from the stream. Please, Fly, try to drink some."

Other dogs stood in the sunlit entrance to the den, their tails tucked low with worry. Meadow wriggled through the little group of watchers, a limp weasel in her jaws. Gently she laid it down before the ailing dog, then licked his ear.

"Can't you eat just a little, Fly?"

The brown-and-white dog didn't reply. His nostrils flared slightly at the scent of food, but he seemed unable to even lift his head. His eyes rolled, showing the whites, and his tongue flopped onto the dry earth beneath his muzzle.

"Maybe it was something he ate to start with," Moon murmured to Meadow. "Maybe that's why he can't eat now?"

"But no other dog got sick," said Meadow, looking troubled. "All the prey has been fresh, and there's been nothing we haven't eaten before."

Moon shook herself in distress. "That's true, but—what?" Her ears pricked and she swung her head. "Why are they barking?"

A volley of alarmed yelps echoed around the glade. Tensing, Moon cocked one ear forward.

Meadow gave her a lick. "I don't know. But if you want to go and look, I'll stay with Fly."

Moon ducked out of Fly's den, past the knot of anxious dogs, and bounded toward the disturbance. Snap, Pebble, and the long-eared black dog Mulch were racing into the camp, their hackles up and fur bristling. Mulch was trembling as he slithered to a halt in the dry leaves.

"Strange dogs," he barked. "Sniffing around our territory!"

"Where?" Alpha trotted forward, instantly alert.

"Over by the stream," growled Pebble. "So they're taking all our water as well."

Alpha made a low huffing sound. "I doubt they'll drink it dry, Pebble, but let's go together as a Pack and see what they're after. We don't want trouble if we can help it, but we don't want a strange Pack muscling in on our territory, either."

"It could be that they're just passing through, and needed to drink," counseled Beta.

"It could," agreed Alpha. "So let's play it cool for now. But we should certainly put on a show of strength, just to let them see our land isn't here for the taking. All dogs in the camp who are not with pup, follow me."

Her Father-Dog and Mother-Dog were so wise, Moon reflected as she trotted at Alpha's heels. Alpha was strong enough to defend the Pack, but he wouldn't place them at risk by picking unnecessary fights. And his mate, her Mother-Dog, was clever and supportive. *Hunter and I can be like that. . . .*

The sky beyond the treetops was heavy with rain, but though the sky was ominous and the clouds dark, it remained dry as the dogs made their way toward the stream. Ahead of Moon, her Father-Dog halted, his tail swishing idly. It was the gesture of a dog who was willing to talk, but who was also sure of his ground and his own strength. Beta moved forward to stand at his side.

The strange Pack stood in front of them, right beside the stream. They were an odd-looking bunch, Moon thought, and there weren't many of them. Her Father-Dog wasn't likely to feel threatened by these interlopers. The one who seemed to be the Alpha was a powerfully built gray creature with yellow eyes—he had more than a touch of wolf blood, if Moon knew anything about those wild, mysterious creatures. At the wolfish dog's side was his Beta, a long-eared, feather-tailed, mean-looking red dog. Close to them was another huge dog, one even bigger than his Alpha: His fur was black and brown, his head heavy and strong and—rather noble, Moon thought. She liked his dark determined eyes, which held no hint of aggression. There were two other black-and-tan dogs, but they were much smaller; Moon thought they looked like littermates. One of them, as he took a limping pace forward, revealed that his foreleg was badly twisted.

Alpha surveyed the newcomers with a stern eye. "Greetings, strangers. What brings you through my Pack's territory?"

The other Alpha didn't answer for a moment. He tilted his head arrogantly, examining the dogs who faced him. He glanced briefly at his Beta, then at his huge black-and-brown Pack-mate with the fierce, kind eyes.

At last he licked his jaws and narrowed his wolfish eyes. "We're not traveling *through* anywhere," he said, with what Moon thought was a deliberate hint of menace. "We are searching for a new territory. This one seems perfect."

Moon heard her Mother-Dog suck in a shocked breath, but her Father-Dog remained calm. His lashing tail, though, grew still. Hunter opened his mouth to speak, but Alpha gave him a stern look, and he fell silent. The strange Alpha began to pace back and forth, displaying his powerfully muscled chest and flanks. His red Beta bared her fangs, the skin of her muzzle wrinkling back to show their deadly sharpness.

Moon could only admire the cool collectedness of her parent-dogs. They were both very still, but their paws remained firmly planted on the ground, and their hackles had risen slightly. The Pack had grown large and strong under their calm, levelheaded leadership, and her Father-Dog never led them into pointless skir-mishes. He had always believed that no dog truly won when the blood of others dogs was spilled. Any fight was a last resort.

But that didn't mean he would back down from one. . . .

"This territory is ours." Alpha spoke coolly and steadily. "We have lived here peacefully for many journeys of the Moon-Dog: for three Ice Winds and four Long Light seasons." He gazed meaningfully around the forest surrounding them all. "But large as our Pack is, we don't take more land than we need. There is plenty of good territory beyond ours, and I know you won't have any trouble finding a place to live. Our Pack will certainly not contest your right to land that doesn't belong to us."

The other Alpha's yellow eyes were unreadable, and he moved not a muscle, but his red Beta sprang forward, her teeth still bared.

"We'll take what territory we think best," she snarled. "It's not your Pack's choice, but our own!"

"That's enough, Beta." The wolfish Alpha snapped at her, the clash of his teeth horribly loud in the heavy silence of the trees. The Beta backed off, but she was still bristling. He gave her one warning glare, then turned back to Moon's father.

"I can smell this land," he growled softly. "I can smell the prey that teems through it. Your territory is by far the richest."

Moon glanced anxiously at her Father-Dog, waiting for his response. What the wolfish stranger said was true; their large Pack, whatever the season, always had more than enough food. Alpha looked as if he was thinking hard, but he still didn't rise to the aggression of the newcomers.

But the red Beta could not, it seemed, contain herself any longer. "We will fight you for this land," she barked, scratching at the earth with her claws. "You have no right to stop us from challenging you, and I don't think your Alpha has the stomach for a fight!"

"I said, *enough*." The strange Alpha—who Moon had decided must be at least half wolf—pinned his ears back and bared his teeth, but he didn't snap at his Beta again. His eyes slanted toward Moon's father, a sharp and cunning light in them. "Beta is impulsive, but what she says is, of course, true. We have the right by Forest Law to challenge you for this land. And if you don't concede the territory, we are more than willing to fight you for it."

Moon felt the other members of her Pack drawing closer to her and her parent-dogs. Snap was at her flank, and she heard a low, constant growling from Mulch and Pebble. Hunter bared his fangs.

"Alpha, we're a peaceful Pack," snarled Rush, "but I don't like these dogs trying to push us around."

"I agree," growled Snap. "There are more of us, and this is our territory. Sometimes dogs have to fight for what's theirs, Alpha."

"Don't worry." Alpha spoke through clenched fangs. "I don't want a battle with these dogs, but if they ask for it, we'll happily give them one."

A chill of excitement and fear swept through Moon's fur as she felt her own hackles rise in anticipation of the fight. Bunching her shoulder muscles, she lowered her head and gave a savage growl at the red Beta. All around, her Packmates were drawing together in their battle line, grim with determination.

"Wait!"

It was the voice of the huge black-and-brown dog, who hadn't so much as growled until now. He paced forward, and dipped his head briefly to his wolfish Alpha.

"If I may speak, Alpha? You told us that our best course would be to take a territory close to this one, and demand that we share the good hunting land in common."

For a long moment, the half wolf watched him with those cold, frightening yellow eyes. At last he nodded slowly.

"Yes, Fiery. Perhaps I did say that."

Despite his size, the dog called Fiery lowered his eyes again in respect, and thumped his tail once. "If these dogs are reasonable, Alpha—and they seem to be—they will agree to your terms. I think they will see the wisdom of your plan."

Moon felt her neck fur lower and her muscles relax as a surge of reluctant admiration went through her. She stared at the big dog. Some of the tension had drained from the atmosphere as the half wolf considered Fiery's words. Moon realized how clever the big dog had been to cool the confrontation without showing disrespect to either Alpha, and making sure his own leader did not lose face. Now he glanced at both Alphas and cleared his throat politely.

"My Alpha thought that instead of being in direct competition, we could all hunt together and split the prey fairly. That would save both Packs a lot of energy and effort, too." He nodded at his Packmates. "We have excellent hunt-dogs, but your Pack knows this territory far better. It would be to every dog's benefit if we work together."

The half wolf was still fixing him with his unsettling yellow gaze, but at last he growled, "Yes. Fiery's right. That was my plan." He swiveled his fierce head back to Moon's parent-dogs. There was still a light of haughty arrogance in his eyes. "Do you agree to my plan? Or shall we fight for the land?"

Moon's Father-Dog did not lower his eyes; he watched the other Alpha coolly. *My Father-Dog knows who averted the fight and devised that plan,* thought Moon with secret pleasure, *and it wasn't that half wolf!*

"My Pack and I will discuss this," her father announced calmly. "We'll make our decision together."

"I thought I was talking to an Alpha." There was a sneer on the half wolf's face, his lips curling back over one corner of his muzzle.

Moon was proud to see that her Father-Dog's hackles didn't even stir. He was unruffled as he growled softly, "*As Alpha* . . . I have learned the value of my Pack's counsel. You will have to be patient while I confer with them."

Moon couldn't help glancing back at the big dog Fiery as she withdrew with the rest of the Pack to a hollow between two over-hanging willows. She felt a rush of gratitude to him for defusing the conflict, and she found her tail was wagging of its own accord. Embarrassed, she dropped her eyes and turned quickly back to her Pack.

"I'm inclined to try this plan, at least," murmured Alpha. "That dog Fiery is a smart one."

"Smarter than his leader," growled Beta dryly, and Alpha gave her an affectionate lick. "We have a lot of dogs to feed, after all, and this Alpha and his two biggest Packmates look like strong hunters."

"But they came to challenge us for our territory!" objected Hunter, his ears swiveling toward Alpha in surprise. "Do we really want them living right next to us? Hunting with us?"

"Better to make an alliance with them, surely?" suggested Moon. "They're aggressive and strong, and I'd rather hunt with them than have to guard our borders against them."

Hunter bristled at her side, his face rigid with disapproval, but Moon found she didn't care—especially when Mulch spoke up in her favor:

"Moon's right," he yelped. "As long as they don't enter our territory, this seems to be the best way for both Packs."

Alpha and Beta exchanged long glances, and Moon waited, quiet and patient. She knew it was their way of consulting each other; the two were so close, a glance could say everything. *I can't imagine it being that way between me and Hunter,* she thought wistfully.

But you never know, she reminded herself. *One day we could very well have a connection like my parent-dogs!*

"Very well." Alpha shook his coat, then lashed his tail as he turned back to the strange Pack. "We agree to this plan. Our hunt-dogs will come to this place next sunup, and yours can meet them here."

The half wolf gave a complacent dip of his head, twitching an ear as if slightly amused. "Good. It's settled. We meet at sunup."

As he began to stalk away, his big Packmate Fiery half turned, his dark eyes meeting Moon's. She thought she saw his ears prick forward as his head gave the tiniest of nods.

A thrill ran between her fur and her skin, making her shake herself in unease. Tearing her gaze away from his, she hurried after her Father-Dog and Mother-Dog.

"I like that Fiery," Alpha was telling Beta, as Moon trotted up alongside them. "He advised his Alpha without showing him a grain of disrespect. And his plan was a clever one."

I like him too, Moon realized, picking up her paws more jauntily. *He does seem clever. And gentle. And kind.*

And their Packs were going to hunt together. . . .

Perhaps Fiery and I can be friends. . . .

CHAPTER THREE

Groggily, Moon lifted her head. The air against her hide was cold and very still, and only a faint light filtered into the den—she could tell that it was early, and the Sun-Dog had not yet stretched and risen. But *something* had woken her. . . .

Alarmed, Moon glanced at her sister. Star was curled up close by, her sides trembling, and despite the chilly air, Moon could feel the heat of her body. When she touched Star's flank gently with her nose, the burning intensity of it shocked her. Star's eyes were almost closed, but she gave a tiny hoarse whimper.

"Star!" Moon sprang to all four paws and bent her head urgently to her litter-sister. "Star!"

Again that awful plaintive whine came from her litter-sister's throat, but it seemed Star couldn't even raise her head, much less respond to Moon's frantic licking.

She's caught Fly's sickness, Moon realized with a plummeting sense of dread. *But Star seems much worse than he did yesterday. This has come on so quickly!*

"Star, I'll get help. Wait here!" She realized as soon as she said it how ridiculous that sounded; Star was clearly incapable of moving a hind leg, and her desperate breathing was shallow and wheezy.

Fear squeezed Moon's lungs as she bounded out through the den entrance and raced to her parent-dogs' den. Her paws skidded, sending up sprays of loose earth and leaves as she plunged into the dimness.

"Mother-Dog!" As she caught her breath, she remembered she wasn't a pup anymore. "Beta! Alpha! It's Star—she is very sick!"

Her Father-Dog turned as her Mother-Dog sprang to her paws. "What, Moon?" he growled. "How sick?"

"Very," she panted. "Worse than Fly yesterday."

Beta hurried out past Moon, her eyes sparking with anxiety. As Moon followed, her heart beating hard, she realized her frantic barking had roused many of the other dogs. They were emerging from their dens, their fur bristling, their expressions bewildered and worried. Snap came bounding over, Omega at her heels, and nosed in concern at the den entrance as Beta and Moon squirmed inside.

Moon wished she could calm her heart. The blood pounding

in her ears felt almost painful as she waited for her Mother-Dog's verdict. Beta was nuzzling Star, who shivered where she lay curled on the den floor. Alpha stood at Moon's shoulder, and she was glad to feel his reassuring solid warmth at her side.

"It's all right, Moon," said Beta at last, giving Star's ear a last gentle lick. "She has a sickness, but I've seen it before. It looks terrible and it's frightening, but dogs always recover from it."

"But she's so hot," exclaimed Moon, looking from her Mother-Dog to Star and back. "And her breathing is so bad. . . ."

"Yes," Alpha soothed her, "but Star's young and strong, like Fly. They'll both get better, I promise."

"Your Father-Dog is right." Beta padded back to Moon and nuzzled her neck. "This invisible enemy strikes sometimes, but it doesn't stay forever. It hurts dogs, but it won't kill them."

"Omega." Alpha twisted his head to give the little snub-nosed dog a commanding bark. "Please bring water for Star. She mustn't get thirsty."

"All right, Alpha." Omega almost rolled his eyes; Moon was sure of it. She'd never liked him.

"And bring more for Fly, too," added Alpha sternly. "Keep watch on these two through the night, Omega. They mustn't run out of water."

This time the little dog's sullen grunt was perfectly audible. Moon twitched an ear in annoyance, but Alpha simply stared hard at him until he'd turned and trotted off toward the stream.

Omega's a lazy, bad-tempered little thing, thought Moon resentfully. *But so long as he does his job and looks after Star, I don't care.* She turned once more toward her litter-sister, unable to repress a low whine of anxiety. Star's lolling tongue looked so dry and pale. And this sickness had struck so quickly. . . . "Alpha, are you sure she—"

"She'll be fine, Moon." Beta licked her anxious face. "Now, don't you think we should give your litter-sister some breathing room?"

Moon took a breath to argue, then sighed it out and nodded. If her parent-dogs were calm about this, then surely she had no need to panic. It was only that she was so unused to sickness, and now Star and Fly had both fallen ill within a single exchange of Sun-Dog and Moon-Dog.

But Beta was right. Crowding into the den around Star certainly wouldn't help her. Taking a deep breath, Moon turned and scrambled out of the den mouth, making herself look calm and confident for the circle of dogs who were watching.

Their tails tapped the ground, their ears quivered, and some of them had their hackles raised at the strangeness and anxiety.

Moon gave them a soft bark as she looked around.

"It's all right," she told them, with more certainty than she felt. "Star's sick, but it's not serious."

Hurrying between Meadow and Rush, she picked up speed and trotted out of the clearing. She didn't wait to answer any of the Pack's urgent questions. Her skin prickled with frustration, but there didn't seem to be anything she could do. *I know nothing about invisible enemies,* she thought. *I can't even help Star! There has to be something I can do for her, but I just don't know what it is. I don't know!*

All she could do was pad on, barely seeing her surroundings or listening to the morning birdsong. An early mist lay in hollows, and the horizon, when she emerged from the trees, was hazily beautiful, blurred with silver-gray dawn light. But Moon's heart was too heavy for her to take any pleasure in it.

She wasn't even especially aware of what her nose was telling her—so she stopped with a sharp jolt when the scents became too strong to ignore. This was the new Pack's territory; indeed, she'd already crossed the line between their lands. Hesitantly, she bent to sniff at a scent-marked stump. The message in her nostrils was wolfish, and sharp with warning.

Yes, I've come too far. She sighed, and glanced over her shoulder. Better turn back now, then. The last thing her Pack needed now was a quarrel with their new neighbors.

But as Moon twisted to pad back the way she'd come, she heard a bark of greeting. She stiffened automatically, but the voice wasn't hostile.

"Hello!" The big dog Fiery bounded to her side.

"I'm sorry . . ." Moon began, dipping her head. "I didn't mean to—"

"Don't apologize." His tongue lolled. "I was hoping I'd see you again soon."

She stared at him, surprised, and he sat back on his haunches, awkwardly scratching at his ear. The huge, powerful dog looked so embarrassed, Moon's heart melted and she let her own tongue loll, grinning.

"All the same, Fiery, I shouldn't have trespassed. I *am* sorry."

"Don't worry." Fiery looked cheerful again. "What's your name? You know mine, after all."

"I'm Moon." She felt shy all of a sudden, and glanced away, back toward her own camp. When she met his eyes again, Fiery was frowning with concern.

"Is everything all right, Moon? I apologize if I startled you. If I was being too forward, I'll leave you alone. I don't want you to be mad at me. If you want me to go—"

She shook her head swiftly. "No! I mean . . . no." She licked her chops. "I'm worried, that's all. My sister, Star. She's sick. Really sick." She took a shaky breath. "My parent-dogs say it's going to be all right but . . . I'm worried, Fiery. She got sick so suddenly."

He didn't tell her not to be silly, and he didn't look impatient as she falteringly explained Star's symptoms. He watched her with concern in his dark eyes, nodding now and again to encourage her to go on.

"It's the heat in her body that frightens me," Moon finished. She realized her voice was trembling.

Fiery got to his paws, his tail thumping strongly. "Listen, Moon. You must try not to worry. I know something that can help with the fever, at least. Follow me?"

She hesitated only for a moment, then nodded. She trusted this dog, she realized, without even having to think about it; it was like an extra instinct that she'd only just discovered. As Fiery put his nose to the grass and set off on some unseen trail, she followed him without question.

He reached the edge of a copse of birch, and halted, nodding. "Here, Moon." Opening his jaws, he tore up a fleshy-leaved plant, roots and all, and laid it down at her forepaws. "My Mother-Dog taught me about this. It'll help bring the heat down in Star's body.

Get her to chew it." He turned to tear up more of the plant with his teeth. "And make sure she has plenty of water. That's important."

Moon stared down at the plants, and then at Fiery. She opened her jaws to thank him, then realized she didn't know what to say. Not long ago she'd been filled with despair; now he'd kindled a new hope in her heart, and the day looked different altogether. She could help Star! Strangely, a part of her wanted to butt her head against his neck and nuzzle him in gratitude. But that was ridiculous. She barely knew the dog! To stop herself from licking his nose, she bent and picked up the plants in her jaws.

"Thank you," she mumbled through them, forcing herself to meet his eyes. "It means—"

"Go on." Fiery nodded. "You'd better get that to your sister."

Without another word—she couldn't think of the right one anyway—she spun on her haunches and raced back to her Pack, and to Star.

CHAPTER FOUR

Whatever happened to that feeling?

It had only been a few journeys of the Sun-Dog since she'd bounded away from Fiery with a new and excited optimism. Now, exhausted, Moon scraped at the earth, digging out clods of it. Every muscle in her body hurt, but it was nothing compared to the pain in her rib cage. It couldn't be her heart, she thought. Her heart had curled up like a sick pup, and died inside her.

I remember the feeling I had then. It was hope, but it's not there anymore. It's gone.

Her paws were clogged and sticky with earth, but the hole seemed deep enough now. She took an exhausted step back, and made herself look at the limp corpse beside her.

Oh, Mother-Dog, you were so wrong.

Mulch and Snap too stopped digging, and watched her. Moon swallowed. Then as gently as she could, she closed her jaws around the body's scruff, and dragged it to the edge of the hole. A tug, and one last jerk of her shoulder muscles, and the body tumbled into the mouth of the Earth-Dog. Moon closed her eyes.

It's only been two journeys of the Sun-Dog since she and Alpha helped me bury poor Star.

Oh Earth-Dog, please take care of her.

Take care of my Mother-Dog.

Moon opened her eyes, but she couldn't bear to look at Beta's lifeless body any longer. Soon there would be nothing but a scar of disturbed earth to show she had ever existed. A scar of earth to go with the others, Moon thought, staring around the glade. Star's grave, close to her Mother-Dog's, and Fly's.

Will there be more? she thought, as grief tightened her throat. *My Father-Dog is sick. Omega is sick. Every other dog is sick with fear. I know there will be more. I can't bear it, but there will be.*

Moon clenched her jaw muscles. She had to bear it. She was Alpha in all but name, until her Father-Dog recovered from this terrible sickness.

And he would recover. He *had* to.

Besides, she berated herself, she was lucky in one way: The strong and reassuring presence of Fiery made a huge difference. Without him, Moon might have curled up in a ball herself, and given up hope. Calm and steady, he organized hunts so that healthy dogs wouldn't go hungry, and he searched out more of the fever plant, bringing jawfuls of it back to Moon's Pack until they had a store of it beneath a cool outcrop of stone.

"It must have come too late for Star and for your Mother-Dog," Fiery had told Moon with sadness. "And this sickness seems to be a very bad one. But at least the leaves can help the other dogs."

It did seem to bring down the heat in the sick dogs' bodies, but Moon doubted that it could heal them now. Fiery's Pack obviously agreed, because they and their Alpha stayed well away from Moon's Pack. Fiery told her the half wolf wasn't very pleased that he was visiting the sick dogs.

"But I won't let you cope with this alone," the huge dog had told her. "I've told my Alpha I can't do that."

Moon was more grateful to him than she could say; but there seemed to be nothing even Fiery could do to save her Pack.

Returning to the present, she looked once more at her Mother-Dog's grave, then shook her head and turned to her companions.

"I can't, Snap," she whined. "I can't bury her."

"It's all right, Moon." Snap gave Mulch a glance, and he nodded.

"We'll cover her with earth," the black dog agreed. "Make sure she's completely with the Earth-Dog. You go on back to the Pack."

Her paws felt as heavy as river-stones as she padded back to the camp. As she passed the small den where Omega lay, his eyes dull and haggard, Moon pushed her nose in. She couldn't help thinking it felt like a grave already—the air smelled so *stale*.

"Do you need anything, Omega?" she asked him gently. "Do you have enough water?"

He could barely nod his ugly little head, but she could see that the strip of bark beside him still glimmered with fresh water. There was nothing she could do for now. *Who'd have thought we'd end up caring for our own Omega?* she thought. *And who'd have thought I'd ever feel sorry for that mean little dog?*

She padded on to her Father-Dog's den. He looked a little more alert than Omega, she thought—but she suspected he was putting on something of a brave show.

"Moon," he growled hoarsely, propping himself up with difficulty on his forelegs. His ribs jutted out beneath his dull coat, and Moon felt a lump of fear in her throat.

"Father-Dog . . ." she said. "Alpha, is there anything you need?"

"Just one thing at the moment, Moon." His eyes held hers, and they were very serious. "I need you to lead the Pack."

Moon gave an involuntary yelp of shock. "No, Alpha! I'm making sure you get healthy again. I haven't got time to . . . You can't make decisions like that just now. You're not well, and—"

"Exactly, Moon. I'm not well. Don't be scared." His mouth quirked with fond amusement. "I've always known you'll make a wonderful Pack leader. You're levelheaded, you have plenty of dog-sense. That's exactly what the Pack needs right now: a dog who won't panic or make rash choices. Please, Moon. Do this for me."

Moon had to pause, breathing rapidly, her heart thumping with anxiety. At last she growled softly, "Yes, Alpha. All right. I'll do my best."

"I know you will, Moon."

She touched her nose to his, and was horrified to feel how hot and dry it was. But there was no time to worry at this moment. Alpha was already turning his head, painfully slowly, to bark as well as he could.

"My Pack, to me! All dogs who are not sick, come to my den."

His head flopped back as Moon heard the sound of dogs approaching: the rustle of grass, the pad of paws on hard earth, the rapid panting of fearful Packmates. With a huge effort, Alpha stumbled to his paws, and with Moon supporting his flank, lurched unsteadily to the den entrance.

The Pack's eyes, Moon noticed, were bright with fear and uncertainty as they gazed desperately at their Alpha. *My Father-Dog is right,* she realized. *They need to be led, now more than ever.*

"Packmates, hear me." Alpha's voice was weak, but in the silence it rang out clearly enough. "For now, I am not able to lead you as I should. My daughter Moon will take my place while we fight this invisible enemy. I ask you all to follow and obey her as you would me. And to give her your wisest counsel, too."

For long moments there was a tense silence. Then, one by one, dogs began to yip their support.

"Whatever you ask, Alpha," growled Pebble.

"Moon is our Alpha until you recover," added Mulch.

"We follow Moon," barked Snap. "She represents you."

Moon watched them all, relieved and pleased at their support. She stepped forward, fighting down her nervousness.

"Packmates, I want us all to howl together," she told them. "We'll howl for those we have lost." *My Mother-Dog,* she thought sadly, *and Star. I should howl for them. But that's not the most important thing. . . .* "And we will ask the Spirit Dogs to guide us, and heal our Packmates. We'll offer them a Great Howl, to ask for strength and health for our Pack."

The dogs formed a circle, and Moon helped her Father-Dog to limp out of his den. She sat close to him, supporting his weak body as the dogs tilted their heads and began to sing out their howls. As the sound rose around her, filling the air, she felt strength and courage seeping back into her.

We've survived many things, she thought, as hope stirred again in her heart. *Surely our Pack can survive this too—if we stay together.* She redoubled her own howls, crying out to her own spirit, the Moon-Dog, even though she was not visible in the morning sky. *She'll hear me, I know she will. She always has.*

As the Howl faded, and dogs shook themselves and turned slowly away to go about their business, her Father-Dog turned to her, and gave Moon a weak lick.

"I knew I was right," he murmured. "Your first act as leader was to bring the Pack together. Well done, Moon."

Her fears began to dissolve in a warm glow of pride. "Thank you, Alpha. I'll do everything I can to lead this Pack back to strength."

But I can't do it alone, she realized, *and I shouldn't! That's what Pack is, after all.*

With the glow of the Great Howl still in her bones, she trotted toward the hunters' den. For the first time, she understood the wisdom of her parent-dogs in choosing Hunter as her intended mate. *I need him now. Hunter loves to lead. He can handle the organization of hunting and patrolling while I tend to the sick dogs.*

Now, at last, we'll learn to be a team!

Hunter was sitting with Rush and Meadow, just outside the hunters' den, and as he glanced toward her, Moon realized again, with a flush of pride and admiration, how strong he was. She wagged her tail as she approached, and opened her jaws to make her suggestion.

Before she could speak, Hunter had gotten to his paws. His expression, as he stared at her, was less than welcoming, and for a moment Moon faltered.

"Moon," he said. "You should be the first to know. Rush, Meadow, and I are leaving the Pack."

Her carefully prepared words caught in her throat. Moon could only gape at him. "What?"

"It's the smart choice," Hunter's voice was cool and unapologetic. "Don't you see? It would be stupid to stick around here and get sick ourselves. We're going to make a new Pack, a strong one, with healthy Packmates. We want you with us, Moon. We'll be

Alpha and Beta, you and I: just as we were meant to be. We'll lead a strong and vigorous Pack without sickness."

Moon wanted to speak, to bark her fury at him, but her throat was too tight with disbelieving shock. Disgust rippled through her muscles, and made her stomach turn over.

At last she managed to choke it out: "You want to abandon the Pack when it needs you most?"

He hunched his powerful shoulders. "It's not a Pack anymore. It's too weak to survive."

Her world was whirling, her brain dizzy with confusion. This didn't make sense!

"You'll even turn your back on my Father-Dog, who promoted you, who was so kind to you?" Moon's bark was hoarse with fury. "I won't leave with you, Hunter. I'll stay where I belong. I will never, *never* abandon my Pack!"

Hunter stared at her for a moment, and she hoped against hope that her words had struck home. Surely he couldn't deny the law of the Pack and the will of the Spirit Dogs? Surely he'd realize he was wrong, see his mistake, change his mind!

But Hunter only turned with a dismissive flick of his tail.

"Then you're a stupid dog," he said coldly. "You'll sicken and die with the others, Moon. Rush, Meadow, and I will live and be strong. Good-bye, Moon, and good luck. Luck's all you've got left to help you now."

And with that last contemptuous growl, he turned and walked away.

CHAPTER FIVE

The Sun-Dog was yawning and settling on the horizon in a blaze of gold as Moon waited for the hunting patrol to return the following day. The beauty of his colors was altogether at odds with her mood. The golden Spirit Dog had traveled a full day's journey since Hunter, Rush, and Meadow had abandoned the Pack. *How could the Sun-Dog let them do this to us?* Sometimes Moon wondered if he even cared about the mortal dogs dashing around on the ground beneath him, struggling to survive in a harsh world.

No, of course he cares, she told herself firmly. *And we have the help of the other Pack; that counts for so much. My Father-Dog was wise to make a hunting alliance with the half wolf.*

She saw that more clearly than ever. After all, her own Pack had now lost every one of its hunt-dogs, whether to sickness, exhaustion or—worst of all—betrayal.

Mulch had fallen ill only yesterday. Snap, Pebble, and Moon

herself were all healthy so far, but all their time and energy went toward tending to the dogs who were sick and helpless.

Moon was sure the half wolf was none too pleased to be propping up an ailing Pack, but so far, their agreement had stood. And that was thanks to Fiery, she realized. He came to their camp every day with fresh prey for the sick dogs. Without his help, Moon knew they wouldn't even have lasted this long.

A twig cracked, and low branches rustled in the line of trees ahead. Eagerly, Moon took a pace forward, hoping to catch her first sight of the returning hunters. If only they'd found good prey today . . .

Her ears twitched and she let out an involuntary growl. Those pawsteps were too light to be the hunting dogs. They were quick and surreptitious, and there seemed to be too many of them. . . .

"Smell dogsies? Sick dogsies!"

"Ohhh, we does, cohort, we does!"

The nasal voices were filled with venom, and Moon's blood ran ice cold in her veins.

Coyotes!

They burst from the trees not two rabbit-chases from her flank: wiry, quick, and savage. For a horrible instant Moon couldn't move; she could only stare in horror, trying to count their grayish-yellow pelts. How many? Ten, twelve?

Too many!

Coyotes were spiteful and vicious. They preyed on the weak, and there were a *lot* of weak dogs in the camp behind her. The coyotes were piling toward the glade now, a tumbling mass of murderous teeth and claws. Wrinkled muzzles snuffling the air, slobber flying from their hungry jaws, they hurtled straight for the dens where the sick dogs lay.

Moon whipped around and raced to intercept them, flinging herself into the path of the leaders. She stiffened her shoulders and lowered her head, snarling, as they slithered to a halt in front of her.

"Back off! Get away!" She bared her teeth.

"Ha! Ha! No! Dogsie run now, dogsie live!" The first coyote lunged for her throat, and she could only dodge back, snapping wildly with her own jaws.

"Snap!" she barked, gasping in air between each desperate bite. "Pebble! Help!"

She couldn't turn to see her friends come racing from their dens, but she heard their pounding paws and their snarling barks. The two dogs appeared on either side of her, biting and clawing at the coyotes, but Moon's relief was short-lived. *There are only three of us. We'll never hold them off!*

A yellow flash caught the edge of her vision and she twisted, sinking her jaws into a scrawny neck. But as she flung that coyote away, another leaped and bit her shoulder hard. Moon yelped, lashing at it with her claws. Beside her, Snap was thrusting violently at a coyote's belly with her hindlegs as another struggled to hold her down.

Moon's sight was blurred with blood, and her lungs felt like they were on fire. She had never fought like this before. There was no time to catch a good lungful of air, or plan a clever tactic. She could only bite and scratch and snarl, flailing wildly at each new enemy that piled on. Her Father-Dog had rarely led the Pack into battle, and then only when he had no other choice. And, while Moon was accustomed to the dog-on-dog challenges for rank within the Pack, those duels were fought with honor. There was no honor here—only a vicious, mindless struggle to kill or be killed.

The coyote that had wounded her shoulder was back; she saw his yellow eyes just before he sank his fangs into her upper foreleg. Yanking herself clumsily from his jaws, she felt her flesh rip, and the trickle of warm blood; she clamped her own teeth on his spine and tossed him weakly aside, but the damage was done. When she lunged for him again, her leg faltered under her, and she stumbled, almost crashing to the ground.

If I fall, they'll kill me.

The realization hit her with a cold, sickening certainty. She could make out Pebble, a few tail-lengths away, and the cruel gash in the black dog's side. Blood was gushing from it in frightening quantities. Snap was almost hidden beneath a pile of coyotes, fighting desperately but gradually subsiding under their numbers. Once the three of them were dead, Moon realized, the coyotes would be free to kill every dog in the camp.

My Pack is dying. My Pack is dying!

"You! Coyote *vermin!*"

Gasping, Moon turned. The furious bark came from her Father-Dog's den. Alpha was standing at its entrance, his leg muscles trembling with the effort, but his muzzle was peeled back to show his fangs. For a moment the coyotes paused, glancing up nervously, and one tumbled off Snap's back.

"You want easy prey?" Alpha barked savagely. "Take me!"

"No!" barked Moon in terror, but the coyotes had already turned to fly at him. Alpha spun and ran, plunging weakly away from the den with at least eight of the coyotes snapping at his heels.

He could barely put one paw in front of the other, and as he lurched and stumbled into a gap between two pines, the coyotes were on him. Teeth flashed and claws raked as they dragged him to the ground.

"Father-Dog!" howled Moon. She bolted toward him, but two of the coyotes had held back, and now they barred her way. They lowered their heads threateningly, lashing their tails and growling their hate.

"Silly dogsy, wait!"

"Yes. We kills Daddy first. You waits your turn, heh!"

Furious, Moon flew at them, but they were fast and strong, and not nearly as tired as she was. Bite and scratch as she might, she could not fling them off and get past. *Father-Dog! My Alpha!*

Pain seared her ear as coyote teeth ripped it. She felt the weight of one of them thud onto her back, and then the rake of its claws in her side, but she could barely focus. She couldn't tear her eyes away from her Father-Dog, motionless now beneath a turmoil of vicious coyotes. There was blood on the ground beneath him. *So much blood.*

And then, quite suddenly, the coyotes were backing away from him, yipping with glee. Alpha did not stir as one of them turned its back and contemptuously kicked soil over his blood-soaked body. Moon, pressed to the ground with a coyote's teeth in her scruff, could not even bark to her Father-Dog; she could only stare in grief-stricken horror as the pack of brutes turned to trot toward the dens of the sick dogs.

The coyote who held her down wasn't even fighting her anymore, sure that she was securely pinned. She heard its rasping, nasal voice through her own flesh and fur.

"Heh. Dogsy. Youse can watch. Watches first, then dies."

Moon closed her eyes in despair. *I don't want to see my Pack die.*

She flared her nostrils, trying to smell the forest through the stench of blood. *There it is.* There was almost a feeling of peace as she made out the scents of pine needles, blowing branches, skittering prey. The breeze was smoky with a hint of Red Leaf.

A wild yelping rose from the dens where the sick dogs lay. *They can smell the coyotes approaching. I don't want to hear it happen. Focus on the forest. . . .*

Moon squeezed her eyes tighter shut. She could smell the rich dark soil, the soil that the Earth-Dog nourished with the bodies of dogs. *It's all right. It's all right. I'll go to the Earth-Dog. I'll see my family.*

A new scent drifted into her nostrils, and her breath caught in her throat. Not the Earth-Dog. A mortal dog, one made of flesh and blood—

Fiery!

She blinked her eyes wide open, just in time to see the big dog himself burst through the tree line into the camp. There were two other dogs at his flanks: the black-and-tan chase-dogs who looked so like each other, Twitch and Spring. All three were howling furiously, their teeth bared in deadly rage as they flung themselves at the coyotes.

The coyotes erupted into panic. Moon felt the teeth of her attacker loosen on her neck, just in time for Fiery to grab its head in his huge jaws. He flung the creature aside; it slammed into a trunk and collapsed lifeless to the ground. Fiery didn't wait to make sure it was dead; he turned on the other coyote that tormented Moon, lashing his claws across its face. Moon knew from the spray of blood that he'd blinded it. It took him only moments to finish it off.

"Fiery!" she gasped, clawing her way out from beneath the coyote's broken body. "The others. My Packmates in the dens. They're sick and helpless!"

He gave her cheek one quick, reassuring lick, and then was gone, plunging toward the dens. Moon was too weak and exhausted to lift her head, but she heard the clamor of panicked coyotes, the squeals and howls as they died, the enraged growls of

Fiery and the barking of Twitch and Spring as they followed him and tore into the attackers.

She saw two coyotes flee, limping, into the forest, but she couldn't chase them. As the racket faded and the glade became still, Moon dragged herself by her foreclaws toward the motionless corpse of her Father-Dog.

She staggered up onto her paws, but she couldn't take a step toward Alpha. Her body felt empty, her heart shriveled to nothing.

My sister, my Mother-Dog, my Father-Dog. My friends. My Packmates. Five journeys of the Sun-Dog, and I've lost them all.

Moon slumped sideways, tipped back her head and released a terrible, ringing howl of grief and loss.

CHAPTER SIX

The den was dark, and it felt so cold. There was no warm body close to hers. *Where is Star?*

As she woke, blinking, Moon felt her body instantly erupt into violent shivering. She shook her head. It felt fuzzy and thick, as if it were full of black storm clouds. She couldn't think straight. She wished she could stop shuddering.

I know where Star is. And my parent-dogs. Her gut turned over. *That's why I feel so terrible. It's grief.*

There was a movement at the den entrance. Snap's muzzle poked inquisitively in, twitching at the stale air.

"Moon?" The Patrol Dog took a few steps into the dimness of the den. "I came to make sure you're all right. I'm so sorry about Alpha. About everything."

Moon opened her jaws to tell Snap she was fine, she'd be all right, she would lead the Pack as best she could. But all that came out was a weak, trembling growl.

"Moon?" There was urgency in Snap's voice now as she lowered her head to touch Moon's nose with her own. Pulling back, she whined in dismay. "Moon, you're boiling hot! You're sick!"

"I'm not hot," Moon croaked. "I'm cold, Snap. So cold."

As soon as she said it, though, she felt a wave of heat, oppressive and unbearable. *I'm on fire. My blood, my hide, everything.* Her jaws fell open and her tongue lolled.

"Pebble is sick, too." Snap's dark eyes were terrified. "Her wounds from yesterday aren't helping."

Moon made a huge attempt to focus her thoughts, to clear the sticky fog in her head. She knew what Snap was thinking, and why her voice reeked of despair: *She's wondering how she can possibly take care of us all. She doesn't know how to cope. . . .*

It was strange, thought Moon, but she herself felt very calm. She remembered the terrible battle yesterday: the moment when she had caught the scent of the Earth-Dog, and had known she was going to join her. Perhaps the worst had happened now, and she was no longer capable of being scared.

Or perhaps it's just the sickness, killing me bit by bit. . . .

It was so hard to care. "Snap," she whispered. "Get some of

those leaves. Fiery's plants. For Pebble and me. To chew."

Snap seemed to be relieved to have something—anything—to do. Turning on her haunches, she scrabbled out of the den and raced away. Moon sank back onto her now dirty bed of leaves.

It's the end of my Pack. We weren't killed by those coyotes. We've been destroyed by an enemy we couldn't even see.

Maybe, Moon thought regretfully, she should have gone with Hunter after all. What use had it been, staying with the sick Pack out of loyalty? It had done her no good. It hadn't helped Snap or Pebble. It hadn't even helped the ones who'd been sick in the first place.

Perhaps we should have gone while we could. We'd have saved what was left of our Pack. Was I foolish not to go with Hunter and the others?

Moon closed her eyes, feeling nothing but a heavy sadness. Her head swam dizzily, and for a moment she thought her mind had drifted loose from her body.

I'm hallucinating, she thought, gazing dully at her Father-Dog. Her Mother-Dog stood at his flank, and Star beside her.

Pack is everything, Moon. Her Father-Dog looked at her kindly. *Pack is sticking together. Pack is taking care of every dog. A Pack abandons no dog.*

Her Mother-Dog stepped forward, touching Moon's ear with

her nose. *If you had left the others to suffer, Moon, you would not have been a Pack Dog at all.*

"Mother-Dog . . ." The sound of her own hoarse voice made Moon blink her eyes open. They felt sticky and sore and hot, and she narrowed them against the sting of the faint light.

There was no sign of Alpha, or Beta, or Star. But another dog stood over her, gently licking her neck fur. A big, reassuring, black-and-brown presence.

"Fiery?" she whispered.

"Don't try to talk, Moon. Here. You must try to chew these leaves. And drink. You must drink this water, it's important."

She felt Fiery's strong nose under her foreleg, coaxing and nudging her until she was half upright. Her body swayed groggily on her forepaws, but she tried to sniff at the withered leaves.

Her stomach roiled. "I can't." The water looked unappetizing, even though thirst was raging in her mouth and throat.

"But you must." He nudged her again, and pulled the curved bark a little closer with his teeth. Water gleamed in it.

"I'm not thirsty." She flopped down onto her side.

"You are, Moon. And you must chew the leaves." His gentle voice was insistent. *Oh, why can't he leave me alone?*

" . . . Leave me alone," she echoed the voice in her head.

"No, Moon, I can't do that." Fiery's tongue caressed her cheek-bone. "It doesn't matter if you don't feel like eating or drinking. You have to do it. For your Pack."

Moon blinked. She remembered imagining her family. Star and Beta and Alpha, all standing together. *Pack is everything, Moon.*

Every muscle and bone in her body hurt as she hauled herself up again. She sniffed at the water, then touched her tongue to it.

At once she realized how thirsty she really was. She lapped desperately, weakly, but the clear cold water slipping down her throat felt like a gift from the Sky-Dogs.

"Good," murmured Fiery. "Now, the leaves. Just one—you can do it, Moon."

In fact she managed to chew and swallow three of the dried-up leaves before she flopped down again in exhaustion. "I can't eat any more, Fiery."

"That's all right. You've done great. They'll help you, Moon, I promise." His tongue licked her ear, gently and rhythmically, soothing her. "There's something else that will help, too. You must sleep now."

She couldn't answer him; her mind felt as weary as her body. Closing her eyes, she let herself go limp. The last thing she felt, before darkness enveloped her, was Fiery's warm flank touching hers as he lay down beside her.

It was a good place. A cool, dark place, one without pain. *Time here means nothing. I think I'll stay. . . .*

She didn't want to swim up from the comforting depths of sleep, but Fiery made her do it. She felt his tongue licking her; heard his low voice urging her back to wakefulness.

Moon whined in protest as the pain returned, but he was insistent. Another drink, another mouthful of leaves, and he soothed her to sleep again. "Well done, Moon. Your Pack needs this. Now sleep."

But you won't let me sleep, she thought miserably as he nuzzled her awake yet again. How long had she slept? She didn't know. She remembered only the wildest blur of dreams, but she knew they had been bad ones, and was glad they were only vague memories.

If only he'd let her sleep for more than a few moments. *Is it only that? That's how it feels. . . .*

Time and time again Fiery nudged her awake, coaxing her to drink and to chew the leaves.

"Do it for your Pack, Moon," he'd say, pawing the water closer.

Each time he roused her, she wanted to bite him, but she didn't have the strength. *Don't wake me again, Fiery. Please don't. Let me sleep.*

But he wouldn't. "One more leaf, and I'll leave you to rest. Just one, Moon. Now the water."

The last time he woke her, though, she remembered her dream clearly. She'd been in the jaws of the Earth-Dog.

I was in the dark and I didn't know which way to turn. Terror clutched her heart as she recalled the nightmare. *She was holding me down. She wouldn't let me go. I couldn't breathe. . . .*

As Fiery pushed the leaves toward her, sickness rose in her throat, and she knew she couldn't touch them again. Couldn't even sniff them. *Never. I'll die if I have to!*

She was grateful Fiery had woken her from that terrible dream, but thanks were not what spilled out of her aching throat. "Why can't you leave me alone? I can't do this, Fiery. I can't! Leave me *be*!"

The big dog stared into her eyes, which felt puffy and swollen. He swallowed hard, and nudged the leaves even closer. There was fierce determination in his face; but she couldn't help thinking she saw something else, too, something gentler.

"If you won't do it for your Pack," he whispered, "then do it for me. Please, Moon. I couldn't bear it if you died."

Her breath rasped in her throat as she stared at him. He was trying to sound stern and bossy, but all she could see in his expression was care, and worry—and affection.

Fiery's everything a dog should be, she realized with a jolt that made her weak heart race. *I'm not grateful to him, no. It's not gratitude at all.*

"Come on, Moon," he murmured. "For me."

She dipped her muzzle to the water, and lapped feebly.

Fiery is what my parent-dogs thought Hunter was. He's strong, and brave, and he's a natural leader.

But he's much more than that. He's much more than Hunter ever was. He's the dog my Pack needed in their worst trouble.

Moon paused in her lapping, and caught Fiery's dark, concerned eyes as he nodded encouragement at her.

He's kind as well as brave. He's gentle as well as strong. And he's something Hunter will never be: He's loyal.

He's not just the dog my Pack needs, she realized with an aching clench of her heart. *He's the dog I need. . . .*

CHAPTER SEVEN

Moon's muscles still felt as weak as a pup's, but she grimly kept digging, her claws raking a shallow trench into the soft earth. *I owe it to Pebble. I was lucky, and she wasn't.*

I lived, and Pebble didn't.

So many of my Pack didn't live, she thought with a wrench of grief. *I'm lucky. Because the Sky-Dogs blessed me, and sent Fiery.*

The awful heat and the freezing cold were gone from her bones and muscles. The sickness had passed a day or two ago, leaving her feeble but alive. And the same, it seemed, was true for her whole Pack—what was left of it. Mulch and Omega had recovered, just as she had.

But not Pebble. Moon glanced at the limp body beside the grave, and swallowed hard. The hole Moon, Mulch, and Snap had dug for their Packmate was next to Star's, and close to the places where Alpha and Beta lay. And Fly, too. *At least they'll be* together when they meet the Earth-Dog.

I've lost so much, but what I have left, I owe to Fiery.

She remembered waking that morning, every muscle in her body feeling as if it was made of fragile twigs. But the heat and the sickness and the pain had been gone. It was Fiery who had brought her through the sickness, Fiery who had given her the will to carry on. And it had been Fiery's face she had seen first, his eyes bright with happiness as he realized the danger had passed. He had licked her face, nuzzled her neck, then trotted out into the forest to find her food and fresh water, a spring in his step that she hadn't seen in days.

But when he'd returned, bringing tender chunks of rabbit-haunch and a new bark-segment brimming with spring water—*No more leaves for you, Moon!*—he had sat down solemnly to watch her eat. And when she'd finally satisfied the hunger cravings that gnawed at her thin stomach, he had broken the news.

"I must leave now, Moon," he'd told her, sorrow in his eyes. "I've neglected my duties to my own Pack for too long . . . I'm sorry."

She'd wanted to protest, wanted to beg him to stay with her for just one more journey of the Sun-Dog—but she couldn't. She understood now, more than ever, that Pack was everything. Fiery had done what he could for Moon—*I owe him my life*—but he had responsibilities that he couldn't ignore any longer.

"I'll miss you," was all she had managed to say.

"I'll come back," he had promised her gravely. "As soon as I can, I'll return and see how you're doing. You and your Pack, of course," he'd added hurriedly, looking a little embarrassed.

Moon was eager for him to return. *When he comes,* she thought, *I won't hesitate, I won't waste time. I'll tell Fiery exactly how I feel.* The thought made her ribs shrink with nervousness, but it had to be done. *I need to thank him properly for what he did. Anyway, I can't just let him go, not now.*

"All right, Moon." Snap interrupted her thoughts gently, bringing her back to the terrible present. "We'd better give Pebble to the Earth-Dog."

Shaking off her reverie, Moon nodded. "Of course." She sighed. "Poor Pebble. I wish she could have made it, too."

Respectfully, Mulch licked the mud from his claws before gripping Pebble's body and rolling it toward the hole. Snap hauled on the black dog's scruff, and Moon pushed, and with just a few hard efforts, Pebble's body rolled and tumbled into its grave, landing with a soft thump. Sorrow stabbed Moon's heart yet again as she gazed down at her dead Packmate. Turning away, she began to scrape soil over the black dog's body.

With her back to the grave, she found she was looking straight at Omega. The little dog sat apart from them, thin and even more wizened than he usually looked. His shoulders were hunched and his eyes were dull and surly. He was still too weak from his illness to help with Pebble's burial, but Moon couldn't help wondering if he was being lazy, too.

I mustn't think that way. We need to learn to live as a Pack again.

Should she be Alpha to the remnants of their once-proud Pack, she wondered? Were there even enough of them left to count as a proper Pack? Four dogs, only three of whom were decent hunters; how could they survive alone?

Though if the half wolf's Pack remains friendly, and if they help us, I think we can manage. . . .

A big shadow moved in the trees beyond the dogs' graves, padding toward them, and Moon felt her heart swell inside her chest. Letting her tongue loll happily, she trotted to meet him, leaving the others to finish burying Pebble. "Fiery!"

His eyes were warm as they rested on her. "Moon. You look so much better!"

She dipped her head shyly. "Fiery, I wanted to say—"

"Listen," he interrupted urgently, and his gaze grew pained. "I need to say something first." He took a breath and averted his eyes slightly, as if afraid to meet hers. "Moon, my Pack is moving on."

She couldn't help her startled gasp. Why hadn't this possibility occurred to her? A wrench of pain silenced her for a long moment, and Fiery lifted his head to gaze at her again.

"The thing is, Moon . . . I thought . . . if you wanted to, that is . . ." He clenched his jaws determinedly. "I hoped you might want to . . . come with us."

She licked her chops, lost for words. Her gut was heavy with sadness. *He's leaving. . . . But he wants me to go with him. . . .*

"Fiery," she began, twitching her ears in distress. "I—I can't do it."

"I wish you would."

His face was so kind, his eyes so full of affection. But, she thought, he must know deep down that she couldn't. *He forced me to get better. He fought for my life, and he did it by reminding me how much my Pack matters. He wants me to be with him, but he knows that I can't.*

"I've promised to lead my Pack, Fiery." She lowered her head. "I can't abandon them."

Fiery sighed heavily. "I think I knew that would be your answer, Moon. I know how you feel about your Pack. I know you have a duty to them, and you won't turn your rump on that." His expression became rueful. "But I had to ask you, anyway. Do you understand?"

Oh, yes, she thought. *I understand perfectly, Fiery.* Misery rising in her throat, she met his gaze. "Why do you have to leave?"

"Alpha—my Alpha, that is—he doesn't like staying in a place where there was sickness. He's worried the invisible enemy is still in the air around here, and he thinks staying would be a bad idea. I can't convince him otherwise, I'm sorry." Fiery's tail tapped the ground in agitation. "He wanted to leave before now, Moon; that's the truth. I asked him to stay, so I could care for you, make sure you recovered."

"Oh, Fiery. And you did. You were so kind." She tried to clear the weight in her throat.

"It wasn't really kindness," he said. "But Moon, now that you're better, I have to obey my Alpha."

Moon lay down on her forepaws. She didn't think she could stand upright anymore without wobbling. This was such crushing news, and she was weak already. And this further proof of Fiery's kindness and devotion made her almost dizzy. "You asked your whole Pack to stay? Just for me?"

"Just for you, Moon," he said quietly.

She swallowed hard, trying not to let her voice shake. "I wish I could repay you, Fiery. I wish I could do what you want. I wish it more than anything, but I can't. My family's gone, and the Pack needs me. This territory—it's all we have left."

"That's what I was afraid you'd say." He nuzzled her jaw. "But I do understand."

. Moon sat up on her forepaws, her eyes brightening. *Why didn't I think of it before?* "Fiery, would you consider staying here?" The brashness of her question made her suddenly shy, and she glanced away. "I mean . . . you could stay here. With my Pack, with me. We could lead this Pack, look after them together . . ."

A look of torment crossed the big dog's noble features. "I can't. Oh Moon, I'm sorry, but I can't. You're bound to your Pack—and I'm bound to my Alpha."

"The half wolf?" Moon closed her jaws on her next words: *But he's so . . . arrogant.*

"He found me when I was a pup," Fiery sighed. "He saved me from a giantfur, and he took me in and cared for me when there was no other dog to do it. I know he seems . . . harsh. But I owe him my life and my loyalty, and I can't abandon him or my Pack. Oh Moon. It seems we're both tied by bonds we can't break."

Moon swallowed, nodding. Despite her disappointment, Fiery's loyalty to the half wolf stirred her affection for him even more. *We can't be together. But that's no dog's fault. We both have duties we can't ignore.*

He's the dog I was meant to be with, I know that. But it can't happen. And in a strange way, she loved Fiery even more for it.

"When do you leave?" She could hardly bear to ask.

"Two more journeys of the Sun-Dog, and then we move on," he told her gently.

She gathered the scraps of her courage. "Will I see you again?"

"We'll pass through your territory on our way," he assured her with another lick. "I promise I'll see you then. And say good-bye." He hesitated, then met her eyes, his own full of sadness. "I'll miss you, Moon."

He turned, his paws heavy as he padded back the way he had come. His head hung low, and as he glanced back once, she saw the longing in his face. Then he vanished into the shadows of the wood.

It's just as well he walked away, Moon thought. Her heart felt like a stone in her chest, and for long awful moments she couldn't move. *I don't think I could have been the one to walk away from him.*

She blinked hard, peering into the darkness of the trees, but he was gone. And after all that had happened, she wasn't sure she could bear this final awful loss.

CHAPTER EIGHT

"*You'll never guess who I found* out there." Snap's voice was full of contempt as she trotted into the clearing, tail lashing.

Moon got to her paws. She'd been expecting to see Snap return from her solitary hunt—with so few dogs in the Pack now, there was no team hunting—but it took her aback to see Snap wasn't alone. There was a dog in the shade behind her, and Moon recognized his burly outline.

Moon's jaw felt loose, and her heartbeat thudded in her throat. He was the last dog she'd ever wanted to see again. Grimly she gritted her teeth and stiffened her shoulders, pacing forward to face him.

"Hunter," she greeted him coldly.

"Moon." His tone was airy. "I'm glad to see that a few of my old Pack managed to survive."

I must not bite him. Moon held on to her temper. "What brings you back here?"

"It's as I said. I'm glad to see the four of you escaped the sickness, but you've taken very bad losses, haven't you?"

Moon didn't answer; she only stared at him.

"So," he went on, "I realized where my duty lay."

"A bit late," growled Snap under her breath, but Moon gave her a glance to quiet her.

"And where does your duty lie *this* time?" asked Moon, with heavy sarcasm.

He hunched his shoulders. "With this Pack, obviously. I've returned to lead you."

Moon looked at Snap, whose jaw was open in disbelief. She stared back at Hunter, but the tilt of his head remained arrogant despite their scorn. "You're serious?"

"Of course I'm serious." He tapped his tail impatiently. "I'm stronger than all of you, and a better hunter. You'd be fools not to jump at the chance."

It was lucky, Moon thought, that Mulch arrived back from patrol at just that moment. Otherwise she really might have bitten Hunter. *How I'd love to take off one of his cocky ears,* she thought bitterly.

Mulch was staring at Hunter too, now, and there was no expression of welcome in the black dog's eyes.

I wonder if Hunter expected a slightly more enthusiastic reception, Moon wondered. The thought amused and cheered her, and she managed to take a deep breath and control herself.

"What happened to Rush and Meadow?" she asked.

"Oh, they got sick," said Hunter casually. "I tried to look after them, but they died anyway."

Moon was too flabbergasted by his light tone to answer him, but Mulch spoke up, his voice dry as a rabbit-bone left in the sun.

"That's funny," he growled, and there was an undercurrent of laughter in his tone. "Because guess who I ran into while I was on patrol? Rush and Meadow are looking very well, for 'dead' dogs. You must have taken better care of them than you thought, Hunter."

Hunter opened his jaws. "I—"

"In fact," Mulch interrupted him, "they told me they'd decided to leave *you*. They snuck away in the night because they didn't like being bossed around like pups—and by a dog who's never led a Pack before. I think the words Rush used were . . . let me see . . . *control wolf.*"

For a moment Hunter looked lost for words. He swallowed hard, looking furious and embarrassed. Then he licked his chops and drew himself up.

"Well, Moon," he said grandly. He'd obviously decided to pretend Mulch didn't exist. "Your parent-dogs always wanted us to lead the Pack together. Their dearest wish was that we should be mates, and I think we should honor that wish. You can be Beta to my Alpha."

Moon took an angry breath. *Beta* to his *Alpha*? She'd actually been enjoying his obvious discomfort, but now he had riled her beyond belief. Her amusement died, and she felt her hackles rise.

"I value loyalty in a leader," she growled slowly, choosing her words with care. "I value loyalty in a mate. You've shown none. Of course I won't accept you as my mate, Hunter." Her voice rose and she almost spat her anger: "I reject you with every part of my dog-spirit."

His ears tightened against his skull, and Moon caught a glimpse of that vicious light in his eyes, the gleam she'd never noticed when her parent-dogs were alive. "Then you're a fool," he snarled.

My parent-dogs always thought Hunter would be a strong leader, because he was a strong fighter. But I don't think they would choose him now, if they'd witnessed his behavior. Any Pack deserves better.

Moon stiffened her muscles and lashed her tail, hiding her aching heart behind a frosty coldness. "I may be a fool. But I will say this: Snap, Mulch, and Omega are my Packmates, and I am their Alpha, but I do not choose for them. It's possible they think I'm a fool too." She turned to Snap, and nodded. "If you three wish to follow Hunter, I won't try to stop you. He's strong; he's right about that. He'll lead you well." The strength of her voice faltered slightly as her gaze moved to Mulch, and then to Omega. "I'm not interested in ordering dogs around, and you should all have a say in what happens to this Pack. You must make your own choices. I won't follow Hunter—not if he was the last dog left in the world— but if you want to go with him, I won't try to stop you."

The three of them glanced at one another, and Moon couldn't help but hold her breath. *Please don't leave,* she found herself begging them inwardly. *I don't want to be the last of my Pack. I don't want to be alone.*

But she wouldn't ever say it aloud. She only licked her jaws nervously as Snap stepped forward.

The tan-and-white dog gave Hunter a cool stare. "I too value loyalty in a leader," she said. "And if my Alpha is true to me, I will give that loyalty back till the day I go to the Earth-Dog." Snap swept her gaze contemptuously away from Hunter, and looked at Moon with much softer eyes. "I will not follow Hunter, and I won't submit to him. He's proven himself a coward and a betrayer. You are my Alpha, Moon."

Mulch sprang forward to Snap's side. He didn't even look at Hunter, but focused his gaze on Moon. "I'm with Snap," he said. "Everything she says is true. You're my Alpha, Moon. I follow you, and no other dog, not as long as you want me in your Pack." For the first time he slanted his eyes at Hunter, who was clenching his teeth in fury. "We're better off without this false dog."

Hunter rose to his four paws, trembling as he glared at the squat little Omega, the last dog to make his choice. Omega twisted his already wrinkled muzzle, and his pink tongue darted out to lick his ugly jaws. He looked very uncomfortable—and no wonder, thought Moon, when Hunter was several times bigger than him—but he spoke firmly.

"How could I trust Hunter?" he whined. Backing away from Hunter's furious eyes, he tucked his tail between his legs, and went on stubbornly. "I couldn't trust you ever again. You'd abandon me in the flash of a rabbit tail. I'm staying with Moon."

Moon closed her eyes briefly, feeling a wave of relief and gratitude wash over her. But as Hunter growled, she opened her eyes again and met his gaze steadily.

"You're pathetic," he snarled at her. "Choices? Omegas don't make choices! Hunt-dogs and Patrol Dogs don't vote for their leaders! Your Pack's mine for the taking. It's my right! Your Father-Dog gave me that right. He chose me to be Alpha!"

"He did not," barked Moon, her fur bristling with anger now. "And if he'd seen how you've behaved, how you let down this Pack, you'd be lucky if he made you his Omega! Alphas don't run away from danger. They stay where they are and protect their Pack!"

"Your Father-Dog wished for *me*—"

"Don't you dare!" Hunter's twisting of her Father-Dog's wishes finally broke Moon's fragile self-control. She lunged for him, jaws wide and lips peeled back from her fangs, and had the satisfaction of seeing him flinch away. He dodged her attack, but Snap and Mulch flew at him from each side, snapping at his flanks, barking their fury.

Hunter twisted and ducked, barking once in fright. Then, abruptly, he bunched his muscles and leaped past Snap, fleeing for the trees with his tail clamped between his legs. Moon's teeth closed with a clash, just shy of his rump, but he gave a startled yelp anyway. Even Omega was prancing behind them, watching from safety but urging them on with high-pitched barks, and Snap and Mulch harried Hunter all the way into the trees.

Moon skidded to a halt as they chased the traitor off. Her blood was pounding and her chest heaving, but nothing had given her so much satisfaction in a long time as the sight of Hunter's fleeing hindquarters. Undergrowth crashed and branches snapped as the panicked dog dived for cover and vanished.

Moon watched Snap and Mulch trot back, eyes shining with glee. She let her tongue loll with merriment. Between Snap's teeth was a ragged clump of gray-brown rump fur.

CHAPTER NINE

With everything that had happened lately, and with the hard Pack work shared among just four dogs, Moon thought that the one thing she should be able to do was sleep. Instead she fidgeted and shuffled on her bedding, tossing and turning. She would have to have a word with Omega; he hadn't chosen the right leaves. He hadn't arranged the bedding properly. He—

Oh, it's stupid to blame Omega. I know what's keeping me awake.

Fiery is leaving tomorrow.

Stretching out her aching muscles, she staggered up onto her paws. Her head pounded with tiredness, but the thoughts and fears raced around inside it like rats, giving her no respite. *Admit it,* she told herself angrily. *You're not just going to* miss *him. The truth is, you can't bear the thought that you might never see him again.*

Silvery moonlight filtered in through the den entrance, edging the overhanging branches with a pale glow. Soon the Moon-Dog would be full, realized Moon, and what kind of a Great Howl could they offer her with such a small and vulnerable Pack? They wouldn't be crying out their joy to the Moon-Dog; they wouldn't be declaring their strength and togetherness. Their voices would be small and vulnerable, lost in the forest.

The Moon-Dog won't even hear us, she thought in despair.

It wasn't just that her heart ached at the thought of Fiery leaving. Without his strong presence nearby, she and her Pack would be prey to all kinds of threats: coyotes, foxes, hostile dogs. How could they even survive?

I should regret driving Hunter away, but I can't. I'm glad he's gone. I think that he might have been the biggest threat of all. . . .

All the same, she, Mulch, and Snap were not the biggest and strongest of dogs; and Omega was next to useless in a fight. If they were left undisturbed, perhaps they could struggle on, living from day to day and taking turns to hunt and patrol. But Moon could not imagine a future in which they'd be left alone. The coyotes might want revenge, and those brutes were only one enemy in a forest full of dangers.

Fiery was our protection. With him gone, we'll have no dog to defend us. What kind of an Alpha am I if I can't protect my Pack?

Utterly dejected, Moon padded to the den entrance and sat

down, tapping her tail as she gazed up at the three-quarters form of the Moon-Dog. Beyond the camp the nighttime life of the forest was busy; there were scuttlings and rustlings, the lonely shriek of an owl, the distant harsh cry of a fox. Moon shivered as the breeze touched her hide, and a ragged sliver of cloud drifted over the Moon-Dog's face.

Oh, Spirit-Dog of mine. I don't think I'm cut out to be an Alpha.

Here in the darkness and the stillness of the night, she could be honest with herself. She hated giving orders. She hated trying to boss the other dogs around. Most of all, she shuddered at the thought of being responsible for them, the thought of knowing that they relied on her decisions for their safety and happiness.

It's too much. Father-Dog, you were wrong about me. I'm no Alpha. Moon gave a huge, miserable sigh. *I was happy when I was doing my job, obeying your orders. Not now when I'm giving my own, and worrying myself sick about whether I've done the right thing.*

She was distraught to think she was letting her parent-dogs down, but she couldn't help it. *I want to be useful to the Pack in my own way. I know you had hopes and dreams for me, Mother-Dog, Father-Dog. But they weren't my dreams. . . .*

She didn't even know if she was right to stay in this territory. Did the invisible enemy really linger here, she wondered? The half wolf might be smarter than she'd thought; perhaps it was stupid to remain in a place that harbored sickness. She was so afraid to leave, to walk away from the only home she'd known . . . but was she being a bad Alpha by making her Pack stay in this place?

I don't know—and that's the trouble. I just don't know!

Moon rose to her paws again and padded out into the glade. She paced to one end of it, where Omega lay snoring in his small den, then turned and paced the other way. Back and forth she padded, her mind a turmoil of indecision.

Do I let down my Father-Dog and Mother-Dog?

Or do I risk letting down all that's left of my Pack?

Gray misty light was beginning to outline the trees as the Moon-Dog loped toward the horizon. Moon heaved a sigh, halting in the middle of the clearing. She twitched one ear, hearing Omega mumble and squeak in his sleep.

My Father-Dog is dead, she thought. *My Mother-Dog is dead. But my Packmates are alive. They're alive, and they need me. But they need me to make the right choice.*

I know what I have to do.

On a knoll just beyond the sunup side of the glade, she could make out Mulch's outline; he'd been on guard through the night, and she saw him stretch and yawn. Moon barked softly to him, and he turned.

"Mulch," she said as he approached with his ears quizzically pricked. "Come with me."

She roused the grumbling Omega, and together they padded to Snap's den. Snap was awake and alert immediately, cocking her head.

"What's up, Moon?"

"I need to talk to all of you." Moon sat down. She glanced at the ground, scratched a mark in it with her claw, then looked up again. Her three Packmates watched her eyes, curious.

"Tell us, Moon." Mulch tilted an ear. "You can ask us anything and we'll follow you. You're our Alpha."

"Yes, I am," she murmured. "And your loyalty means everything to me. But this is something I won't do without your consent. Alpha or not, I won't force you into something you don't want. But I have a proposal to put to you all. . . ."

The grass was damp under their pawpads as the four dogs made their way over the ridge that marked the boundary of their land. Moon paused, her claws touching the line she knew was the border.

On the horizon, the Sun-Dog was rousing himself to lope into the sky; his brilliant golden eye blinked over a faraway hill, lighting up the gray dawn landscape with green and gold and pink.

Moon took a breath, gazing out at the shallow expanse of the valley. The clearness of the sky seemed like a good omen; it was a good day to take such a momentous step.

At least, she hoped so. Setting her jaw, Moon took a step over the boundary.

Behind her, Snap, Mulch, and Omega followed, sharing nervous glances. Moon didn't look back at them, though; she had caught the first scent marker on the still air.

"This way," she said, putting all the confidence she could muster into her voice. She trotted determinedly up the slope to the edge of a cleft in the ridge.

There, poised on the highest point and watching the land beyond, was the red Beta. Moon swallowed.

Oh, it had to be her, didn't it? she thought dryly. Shaking herself, she trotted toward the Beta, giving a low friendly bark.

The Beta spun in shock, her face agitated. "You!"

"Beta." Halting, Moon dipped her head respectfully.

"What do you want?" The red dog sounded flustered—as well

she might, thought Moon with inward amusement. She'd been so busy watching the outer territory, she hadn't seen Moon and her Pack approach from her flank.

"We're not here to make trouble," Moon assured her quickly. "I'd like to speak with your Alpha, if I may?"

"Why?" asked the Beta sharply. "We're leaving soon. When the Sun-Dog rises above those trees, we'll be gone."

"I know." Moon made her voice humble. She disliked this dog, but for her Pack's sake, it was important to show deference. "I only want to talk to your Alpha. I—well, my Pack and I . . . we have a proposal for him. I'd be grateful if you would escort us."

The Beta looked annoyed, but she could hardly refuse such a polite request. She sat on her haunches, gave her ear a vehement scratch to express her feelings, and then nodded sharply.

"Very well. I'll take you to Alpha. But don't waste his time! We have a busy day ahead of us."

Quietly amused at the Beta's irritation, Moon followed her down into the valley. The red dog's tail was raised self-importantly as she led them through a cleft between two rocks. The passage opened into a shallow bowl-shaped glade, where dogs rose to their paws to stare at the newcomers.

Moon ignored their curious mutterings and growls. She kept her focus on the half wolf, who paced arrogantly forward from a rock in the center of the camp. When she dared go no farther, Moon stopped, and dipped her head, lowering her tail.

"What's the meaning of this?" growled the half wolf, lashing his bushy tail. "Have you come to challenge me for the leadership of my Pack, Moon?"

There was a ripple of amused growling that fell silent as the Alpha gave his Pack a sharp glare.

"No, Alpha." Moon swallowed, and met his eyes. There was a big, familiar shape at his flank, but Moon couldn't look at Fiery. *I mustn't*, she thought. *Though I really, really want to.*

"This dog says she has a proposal for you." The red Beta's tone was sneering.

"Let me hear it, then." Alpha cocked his ears, curling his muzzle just a little.

"Alpha," said Moon quietly, "my Pack is small. We lost so many to the sickness that attacked us."

"There's barely enough of you to count as a Pack," muttered the Beta, but she shut her jaws at a fang-baring from Alpha.

"We're all healthy now," Moon went on hastily. "But though we're loyal to one another, we can't function as a true Pack."

"But you are their Alpha," pointed out the half wolf, a thoughtful gleam in his eye.

"Yes, and I have no desire to be one." Moon kept her voice steady. "I want to relinquish my leadership. My last act as its leader would be to submit my Pack to you. If you'll have us . . ." She licked her jaws, and lowered her eyes. ". . . Alpha."

There was such a long and heavy silence, she was afraid that the half wolf was going to refuse her. Moon was aware that Fiery was very still and tense, his muscles trembling slightly, and she realized he was holding his breath.

If the half wolf rejects us, I will accept that. I won't beg. I'll walk away with my Pack's pride intact. I don't know how we'll manage, how we'll survive, but we will leave with our heads held high.

Determinedly, Moon finally raised her eyes to the half wolf. He watched her a moment longer, then slid his gaze to Fiery. Finally, he looked back to Moon and nodded.

"Very well," he growled at last. "Work hard, obey my orders, and you are welcome in my Pack."

A wave of relief washed through Moon, making her almost dizzy. "We will. And thank you. *My Alpha.*"

There was a yelp of joy, and Fiery bounded forward. All of Moon's nervousness and uncertainty melted into happiness as the huge dog shouldered the red Beta aside and hooked his head over Moon's neck, nuzzling her and growling with delight.

"Welcome, Moon. To you and your Pack. You've made me happier than I can say."

CHAPTER TEN

Blissfully, Moon stretched her paws, basking in the rays of the Sun-Dog, which warmed her fur. In her moments of relaxation she loved to watch the life of her new Pack bustling around her. Snap lay talking quietly to a lean chase-dog named Dart; Mulch was comparing hunting tactics with Twitch, who was demonstrating his techniques for pouncing despite his bad leg. Omega had been disappointed to find himself at the bottom of the ranks in this Pack, just as he'd been in the old one, but he had settled into his work anyway, although with a rather bad grace. Moon watched as he dragged the old bedding from Beta's den, his expression grumpy. *But then it always is,* she thought with reluctant fondness for the ugly little dog.

It had taken them several hard journeys of the Sun-Dog to reach this new territory, but it was a good one. Moon was surprised by how comfortable she felt, not just in the new land, but with her new Packmates. The sheltered valley felt like home already. The prey was plentiful, with rabbit warrens nearby and a forest that teemed with life. A freshwater stream ran within their boundaries to a broad, glittering lake; they would certainly never go thirsty.

I hope this will be our permanent home, Moon thought dreamily. *At least, I hope we can stay here as long as my old Pack lived in their territory. That was a good life. But this will be, too. I'm sure of it.*

The new Pack could never replace her family, and she still missed Star and her parent-dogs with a constant aching regret. But they were safe in the paws of the Earth-Dog, she knew; and this Pack was the next best thing.

Best of all, she was certain that her Mother-Dog and Father-Dog would have approved of her new mate. Fiery was everything they had both admired in a dog: strong, courageous, kind. *I think if you could see me, Father-Dog, you wouldn't be sorry that I'm not with Hunter. I know you'd be glad I made the choice I did. . . .*

She blinked, sighing. As for her other choice . . .

Well, she had a feeling her Father-Dog would understand that, too. This wasn't what he'd planned for her, but it was what she'd wanted, and it was what suited her best. *I'm lead Patrol Dog.*

I have responsibilities, important ones. That's what matters. I don't have to be Alpha to serve my Pack.

Moon's heart swelled with pride and happiness. *Yes, I think my Father-Dog and Mother-Dog would be very happy with me.*

And I'm happy too. Happier than ever, today . . .

She pricked her ears as she heard the sounds of the returning hunters. Jumping to her paws, she trotted eagerly to meet them. Fiery was in the lead as the four hunters padded into the clearing; his jaws were clamped around a fat squirrel, but he dropped it to greet Moon happily, licking her jaw and nuzzling her neck.

"Fiery," she murmured. "I'm glad you're back. The hunting was good, then?"

"Very good," he told her. "This is fine land, Moon."

"Spring looks a bit uneasy." Moon glanced over his shoulder, curious.

"Yes, but not about the hunting. She was complaining about some bad feeling in her fur. She says her bones are buzzing. I felt it myself, but it's nothing. The air feels a little strange, that's all. I think maybe there's a big storm coming, but it's nothing to worry about."

"I'm not worried." Moon couldn't help panting with happiness, and her tongue lolled with joy. "Fiery, I've got something to tell you."

Instantly, he was all concern. "What is it, Moon? Is everything all right?"

"Everything's better than all right," she told him softly. *Oh, I wanted to prepare him more for the news, but if I don't tell him, I'll burst.* "We're going to have pups."

Fiery jolted back so that he could stare into her eyes. He looked utterly startled, but his jaws opened in a broad grin. "Moon! Really?"

"Really." She turned her head to nuzzle her flank. "I was hopeful yesterday, but now I'm certain. You're going to be a Father-Dog, my love!"

He gave a howl of delight, then fell to licking her ears and nose with enthusiasm. "Moon, this is wonderful! I'll take good care of you, you'll see. I'll protect you through this storm, I'll find you the best prey, I'll—"

She laughed, nuzzling him as they walked together back to their den. "I know you will. And you're going to be a wonderful Father-Dog, I know that too."

I thought I would never be happy again, she thought to herself. *Back when I was sick, and my Packmates were dying, I thought there was nothing left that I could live for.*

How could I have been more wrong? I'm happier now than I've ever been.

"You have time to rest before prey-sharing," Fiery told her. "Are you comfortable, Moon? Are you warm enough? Can I—"

"I'm fine," she laughed gently. "I couldn't be better, Fiery."

As they settled in the den, Moon nestled against Fiery, feeling his warm heartbeat through her flank.

Everything will be good from now on, she thought. *Some mysterious prickling in Spring's hide and bones can't change that. If there's a storm coming, however big, we'll survive it. We can survive anything together, Fiery and I . . . and our pups.*

She closed her eyes, feeling happiness wash over her in a warm tide.

The worst is definitely over.

CHAPTER ONE

Pausing as she stepped out of the forest's shade, Storm took a moment to stretch her paws and her back, and to claw the ground blissfully in the rays of the morning Sun-Dog. His light shone warm on her sleek back and, in the rippling grass around her, he kindled rich scents of rabbits, mice, and squirrels. Storm sniffed appreciatively at the soft breeze. There were good prospects for their hunting patrol.

Storm felt full of optimism on this glittering New Leaf day. It was her first chance to be in charge of a hunt, and she was proud that her Pack Beta, Lucky, had shown such faith in her. *He always has,* she thought gratefully. She owed so much to the golden-furred Beta who had once been a Lone Dog.

She glanced over her shoulder at the team she was leading. *Some of the Pack's best dogs,* she thought with pride. Snap, who had long been part of Sweet's Pack, had always been a fine hunter, and Mickey, despite his Leashed Dog origins, had learned to track down prey with the best of the W

had been one of Blade's Pack, and h

accuracy were invaluable assets. And V

of the mad dog Terror's underlings . . . we

please his leaders and prove his worth, now th

by Terror's horrible threats.

They were an unlikely combination, but that was what m

Storm happiest. Before her own birth, the Earth-Dog had shaken

in the Big Growl. If that had never happened, the Packs repre-

sented in her hunting party would never have come together as

one. After all, Mickey and Snap had come from very different cir-

cumstances—Snap from Sweet's Pack, which had once been the

half wolf's Pack; and Mickey from his home with longpaws—but

that was before the Big Growl had destroyed the city, changed

the world, and forced every dog to fend for himself. Now they

all worked together despite their differences, all of them bringing

their own strengths and skills to their new, united Pack.

Storm had never quite understood why Lucky was always

barking back to the Big Growl. Yet now that she had lived

through a great battle—the one they called the Storm of Dogs—

she saw clearly why the disaster of the Growl meant so much to

him. When a dog had lived through such a world-changing shock, it did affect everything: the world beneath her paws, the scents in her nostrils, each sound that reached her pricked ears. Everything held new significance—and not just potential threat and unexpected danger, but fresh possibilities, too.

Prey had been thin and hard to catch throughout the long Ice Wind season, but now buds were popping into life on the trees, small leaves grew thick on the bushes and shrubs, and the meadows were green with new life. Storm was determined that today's hunt would be swift and successful. "Try that hollow, Storm." Mickey's kind voice was in her pricked ear, and it set her fangs instantly on edge. He and Snap had been trying to advise and guide her all morning, when it was Storm herself who needed to make the decisions. Couldn't Mickey understand that?

"There, see?" the black-and-white Farm Dog went on, oblivious as Storm ground her jaws in frustration. "The hollow beyond the hill." He nodded in the direction of the far side of the shallow valley, toward a dip in the grassy ground circled by young birch saplings.

"Yes, that might be worth a try," Storm managed to growl.

"We can surround it easily and drive out the prey," Mickey went on. "The creek runs close to it, and there's a rabbit warren there."

"I know that, Mickey," said Storm sharply.

Mickey pricked his ears in surprise, then licked his jaws. "Did I say something wrong, Storm?"

"It's just that—" Noticing the slight hurt on his face, she softened, and gave her old friend a lick. "Sorry, Mickey. I'm just a bit preoccupied."

He was only trying to be helpful, after all—and Mickey, along with Lucky, had been one of the dogs who had rescued her and her two littermates when they were helpless, abandoned pups. He'd always looked out for her.

But I want to be able to prove myself. *If they'll let me . . .*

Snap was the next to trot over and push her narrow snout in. "I'm not sure about those high trees, Storm." Her head tilted as she stared at the horizon. "Rabbits could duck around them, and we'd be blocked at several points."

Storm somehow managed to hold on to her temper, though the urge simply to run and hunt was growing unbearable. Her paw pads ached, as if she'd been walking over rough stone, and she wanted to be moving now, not standing still. She could already see distant tawny flashes through the grass. The unwary creatures weren't alarmed—yet—but the dogs would have to move quickly once they were nearer to the warren.

"I think we can cope with the trees, Snap," Storm told her in a low voice. "Let's head toward the hollow, but keep our noses sharp for other prey on the way. We can't rely on catching enough rabbits for every dog."

She reminded herself sternly that Snap and Mickey were her seniors in the Pack hierarchy. *Though I wish they didn't treat me as if I'm still that vulnerable pup Mickey and Lucky rescued.* She gave a silent inward sigh, then nodded at her patrol.

"I want to plan ahead of time, so that we don't have to make a sound later. Arrow and Snap, when we're closer to the warren, you circle around toward the creek. If the rest of us take points between the warren and the wider plain, the rabbits will have nowhere to go. We should manage to take two or three. Stay low, and remember to watch for other prey." With a nod that Storm hoped showed both respect and quiet authority, she led the patrol carefully toward the line of aspens on the horizon.

All the dogs were alert now, placing their paw pads with care and keeping their bodies low, but Whisper slipped past the others to stalk at Storm's side. She gave the young dog an inquisitive glance.

"I think this is a brilliant strategy, Storm," said Whisper, in a low but enthusiastic growl. "You're a great hunt leader!"

"Thanks, Whisper," Storm told him, pricking her ears in slight surprise. "I'd really like to lead the hunt more often, so let's hope this goes well."

"Oh, I'm sure it will. So what else do you think we'll find? Maybe a deer!"

Storm gave a huffing sound of amusement, and shook her head briefly. "I doubt we'll be that lucky, but let's stay alert."

"You always do," said Whisper. There was a light of adoration in the gray dog's eyes, and Storm looked away, trying to keep her focus on the careful stalk-and-slink of the hunt.

A ripple of unease traveled between her fur and her skin. Whisper had treated her with something close to hero-worship ever since Storm had killed Blade, the Fierce Dogs' vicious leader, in the great battle last Ice Wind. Storm had had to do it—and she'd been glad to do it, after all that Blade had done to her litter-siblings and to her Packmates—but the days of battle were over. She was a hunter now.

She hoped Whisper wouldn't always be bringing up the dreadful Storm of Dogs, and Storm's role in it. They had a new life to look forward to now, and Storm was determined to play her part in making it one of peace and plenty for the Pack. It had taken her so much time and effort to live down her reputation as a savage Fierce Dog, a struggle made far harder by the hostility of their old half-wolf leader, Alpha. She didn't want to have to go through all of that again.

Storm raised her muzzle to test the wind direction, pausing with one paw lifted.

Forest-Dog, if you'll listen to me as you listen to Lucky, grant us good New-Leaf prey today!

Her optimism returned as she leaped easily over a small tributary of the stream, enjoying the sleek movement of her muscles and the springiness of the earth beneath her paws. Every sense in her body felt awake after the long, hard Ice Wind, and a slight flash of movement at the corner of her eye sent her twisting in pursuit almost without a thought.

The squirrel shot up the trunk of a tree, panicked, but Storm's snapping jaws found their target. Crunching down, she felt the brittle bones of its body through the scrawny flesh. *Skinny,* she thought, *even for a squirrel. Ice Wind has been hard for every creature.*

Her swift kill, she realized, had served as a signal to the others: the hunters bolted into the chase. Arrow sprinted across a dry streambed, sniffing and searching without luck, but Mickey and Snap began to work together at the foot of a gnarled oak, digging in showers of earth until their paws and muzzles were filthy. Just as Storm bounded to join them, they unearthed a nest of mice. As the tiny creatures skittered in panic, blinded by the light, the two hunters pounced and bit and snapped till they'd created a pile of tiny corpses.

"They're barely a mouthful each," said Snap, pawing at them.

"Every mouthful feeds the Pack," Storm reminded her, pleased. "Well done!"

Her praise, though, seemed to fly straight above Snap's head. The tan-and-white dog pressed her head to Mickey's, and for a moment the two successful hunters rested, panting, rubbing their muzzles affectionately together and licking each other's dirty ears. With a surprised prick of her own ears, Storm took a few paces backward.

Is this really the moment for snuggling up to your mate? she thought with a shiver of puzzled distaste. *What a silly waste of time. It's only a couple of mice, for the Sky-Dogs' sake.*

Turning her rump on them, she snatched up her squirrel and dropped it into the hole Mickey and Snap had dug out at the base of the oak. It was as good a place as any to store their prey till they'd finished their hunt: a deep gap between two thick roots. As she raised her head, a light, warm breeze moved through the trees, bringing with it that tantalizing scent of rabbit. Storm shook off her moment of discomfort. *We're downwind of the prey—this is a good beginning!*

Excitement rose in her once again, and she gave a low commanding growl to summon the others. She felt a spark of pride, swelling to a warm glow, when they answered her call at once. The four dogs fell in at her flanks and followed her lead as she prowled forward, closer and closer to the shallow bowl of land.

The rabbits must be hungry after the long cold, Storm realized: they had still not noticed the patrol's approach. They were too busy browsing and tearing at the new grass with their blunt little teeth. *We should be able to cut them off from their burrows*, thought Storm, *if we all play our part*. Her heart beat fast in her rib cage with anticipation.

Lowering her sleek body still closer to the earth, she crept forward, nodding to the others. They were all in place, just as she'd directed them; again she felt that frisson of satisfaction in her leadership. When she finally sprang, hurtling into the hollow, every nerve in her body sang with the joy of hunting, with the certainty of her own speed and strength and skill. She felt her blood racing, the flex and stretch of each muscle as she dived and dodged and leaped in pursuit of the terrified rabbits. It was like pure energy and fire running through her. *Is this how Lightning of the Sky-Dogs feels?*

And it was working just as it should. White bobtails flickered all around the hollow, and the panicked creatures were scattering straight into the jaws of the waiting hunters. Mickey's powerful teeth clamped down on one of them, and he shook it violently as another doubled back and fled from him—straight into the jaws of Storm. Panting, Storm flung down its limp corpse, then took a moment to watch as Whisper drove the fattest rabbit of all toward the waiting Arrow.

Arrow was loping along on exactly the right line, and Storm could see he would intercept the fleeing rabbit with ease. So she was stunned to see Whisper's head flick to the side. Mid-stride, he veered away slightly and herded the rabbit in a different direction, toward Snap.

But Snap wasn't watching; she was too busy chasing down a dark-furred rabbit of her own. Whisper's rabbit crossed her field of vision just as she was about to pounce on hers, and Snap's pace faltered in surprise and confusion.

Arrow was racing furiously after the rabbit now, but the abrupt change of tactics had spoiled his line and his focus. Both rabbits, the dark-furred one and the lighter one Whisper had been driving, bolted straight between Arrow and Snap, and vanished into their burrows with a flash of two white tails.

Storm raced toward them, but she knew she was already too

late. Skidding to a halt in a flurry of sandy earth, she stared at the dark burrow entrances, swamped by frustration and anger. Behind her Arrow and Snap had drawn up too, snapping their drooling, empty jaws.

As Whisper bounded to a faltering, shamed halt between them, Storm turned on him.

"Why did you do that?" she barked furiously. "We lost two good rabbits!" *And more*, she realized. In the confusion of Whisper's mangled hunting attempt, several other rabbits had reached the safety of their warren.

"That was the fattest rabbit!" added Arrow in an angry snarl. "Those two would have fed three dogs between them!"

"What were you thinking? Were you thinking *at all*?" Storm laid her ears back and growled furiously at Whisper.

The dog ducked his head, lowering his forequarters and shuffling forward, his tail clamped down tight. He looked as if he wanted to sink right through the earth and join the rabbits underground.

"I'm sorry, Storm," he whined miserably, blinking and flattening his ears. "I didn't mean to . . . I thought . . . I just meant . . ."

Storm gave her head a violent shake. "*What*? What did you mean?"

"I—" Whisper's glance flicked quickly toward Arrow, then back to the ground.

"Don't be hard on him, Storm." Snap took a pace forward, and nodded at the unhappy Whisper.

Storm turned to her, surprised at the hunt dog's tolerance. "He spoiled your hunt too, Snap."

"Look, Storm, it's obvious." Snap tilted her head and sat down, curling her tail around her haunches. "Whisper was nervous of Arrow. He doesn't like hunting with him, and to be honest? I understand why. I don't blame Whisper."

Storm stared at Snap's cool expression, her jaw loose. "What?"

"After all we went through with the Fierce Dogs, it's hard for us to trust any of them." Snap hunched her thin shoulders. "I know Arrow's in our Pack now, but it's hard to treat him as a true Packmate."

Not knowing what to say to that, Storm turned to Arrow. His short black fur bristled along his shoulders and spine, and resentment oozed from him, but the Fierce Dog said nothing. He licked his jaws angrily, and looked away. Then he padded across to one of the dead rabbits, picked it up in his powerful jaws and paced in the other direction.

And what do I do now? Snap wasn't being fair, and this felt so wrong to Storm. *Just when I was thinking how good it was that we were united, that members of all Packs were working together.*

But if she spoke up for Arrow, Snap would think she was only siding with her fellow Fierce Dog. She might even accuse Storm openly of favoring her own kind, of being Fierce Dog to her core. *What might she say aloud—that I'm ruled by my bad blood?*

"You all trust me," she said at last, staring at her Pack-mates. Snap, Mickey, and Whisper looked so resolute, and Storm's head spun with confusion. "You trust me, and I'm a Fierce Dog too. Just like Arrow!"

Mickey caught Snap's eye, and Storm saw a look pass between them, one that she couldn't quite read. Snap's ear flicked once, dismissively. Then, tentatively, Whisper gave a soft growl.

"You're not like Arrow," he mumbled. "You're different." He glanced at Snap and Mickey. "Storm's different, isn't that right? She killed Blade!"

Storm stared at him, open-jawed. With a crawling sense of horror, she realized that Whisper's eyes were fixed on her again, worshipful.

She shook herself, dumbfounded. "Let's gather the prey," she told them. "What there is of it." Gazing dismally at the pitiful haul of rabbits, she felt a crushing sense of disappointment. Her hopes had been so high for her first time as hunt leader. "We'll try another spot before we return to the camp, but we'll have to go some distance. All the prey around here will have heard us by now."

"Of course, Storm." Whisper got quickly to his paws and trotted after her like a devoted pup.

As she led the small patrol farther from the cliffs and the Endless Lake, heading for a far belt of pines, Storm's stomach squirmed and her fur prickled. She'd begun this hunt with such high hopes and excitement, yet now they were returning with a poor prey-haul—and a bunch of dogs who didn't, after all, want to work together as her perfect team.

Is that terrible battle the only thing they care about? If I hadn't killed Blade, would they trust me at all? Or would I be just another Arrow—alone in a Pack that thinks I'm the enemy?

ERIN HUNTER

is inspired by a fascination with the ferocity of the natural world. As well as having great respect for nature in all its forms, Erin enjoys creating rich, mythical explanations for animal behavior. She is also the author of the bestselling Warriors and Seekers series.

Visit the Packs online and chat on Survivors message boards at www.survivorsdogs.com!

FOLLOW THE ADVENTURES!

WARRIORS: THE PROPHECIES BEGIN

In the first series, sinister perils threaten the four warrior Clans.
Into the midst of this turmoil comes Rusty, an ordinary housecat,
who may just be the bravest of them all.

HARPER
An Imprint of HarperCollinsPublishers

www.warriorcats.com

In the second series, follow the next generation of heroic cats as they set off on a quest to save the Clans from destruction.

HARPER
An imprint of HarperCollinsPublishers

www.warriorcats.com

1 — THE #1 NATIONAL BESTSELLING SERIES
POWER OF THREE
WARRIORS THE SIGHT
ERIN HUNTER

2 — THE #1 NATIONAL BESTSELLING SERIES
POWER OF THREE
WARRIORS DARK RIVER
ERIN HUNTER

3 — THE #1 NATIONAL BESTSELLING SERIES
POWER OF THREE
WARRIORS OUTCAST
INCLUDES A SNEAK PEEK AT ERIN HUNTER'S NEW SERIES: SEEKERS #1: THE QUEST BEGINS
ERIN HUNTER

4 — THE #1 NATIONAL BESTSELLING SERIES
POWER OF THREE
WARRIORS ECLIPSE
ERIN HUNTER

5 — THE #1 NATIONAL BESTSELLING SERIES
POWER OF THREE
WARRIORS LONG SHADOWS
ERIN HUNTER

6 — THE #1 NATIONAL BESTSELLING SERIES
POWER OF THREE
WARRIORS SUNRISE
ERIN HUNTER

In the third series, Firestar's grandchildren begin their training as warrior cats. Prophecy foretells that they will hold more power than any cats before them.

NE
LOC
COMIN
SOO

HARPER
An Imprint of HarperCollinsPublishers

www.warriorcats.com

In this prequel series,
discover how the warrior Clans came to be.

These extra-long, stand-alone adventures will take you deep inside each of the Clans with thrilling adventures featuring the most legendary warrior cats.

HARPER
An Imprint of HarperCollinsPublishers

www.warriorcats.com

WARRIORS: BONUS STORIES

Discover the untold stories of the warrior cats and Clans when you download the separate ebook novellas—or read them in two paperback bind-ups!

WARRIORS: FIELD GUIDES

Delve deeper into the Clans with these Warriors field guides.

HARPER
An Imprint of HarperCollinsPublishers

WARRIORS: MANGA SERIES

The cats come to life in manga!

HARPER
An Imprint of HarperCollinsPublishers

www.warriorcats.com

ALSO BY ERIN HUNTER:
SURVIVORS

SURVIVORS: THE ORIGINAL SERIES

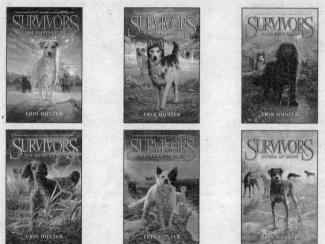

The time has come for dogs to rule the wild.

SURVIVORS: BONUS STORIES

Download the three separate ebook novellas or
read them in one paperback bind-up!

Paperback

HARPER
An Imprint of HarperCollins Publishers

www.survivorsdogs.com

ALSO BY ERIN HUNTER:

SEEKERS: THE ORIGINAL SERIES

Three young bears . . . one destiny.
Discover the fate that awaits them on their adventure.

SEEKERS: RETURN TO THE WILD

The stakes are higher than ever as the bears search for a way home.

SEEKERS: MANGA

The bears come to life in manga!